The Lost Woods

The Lost Woods

STORIES

H. William Rice

The University of South Carolina Press

© 2014 University of South Carolina

Published by the University of South Carolina Press
Columbia, South Carolina 29208

www.sc.edu/uscpress

Manufactured in the United States of America

23 22 21 20 19 18 17 16 15 14   10 9 8 7 6 5 4 3 2 1

Library of Congress Cataloging-in-Publication Data

Rice, Herbert William, 1952–
 [Short stories. Selections]
 The lost woods : stories / William Rice.
     pages cm
   ISBN 978-1-61117-329-1 (Hardbound : alk. paper) — ISBN 978-1-61117-330-7 (Ebook)
 1. Title.
   PS3563.O8749A6 2014
   813'.54—dc23

                                                        2013041125

This book was printed on a recycled paper with 30 percent postconsumer waste content.

For sons Will and Matt and my brother Dan

In memory of my father, the Reverend Herbert W. Rice,
   who took me hunting and told me stories

CONTENTS

ACKNOWLEDGMENTS

Grateful acknowledgment is made to publications where versions of these stories or portions thereof appeared. Earlier versions of "Stalking Glory," "The Longing," and "Uncle Ivory" appeared in *Gray's Sporting Journal*. An earlier version of "The Honor and Glory of Hunting I—Luke" appeared in *Gray's Sporting Journal* as "Early Lessons." An earlier version of "My Uncle's Dogs" appeared *in Gray's Sporting Journal* as "My Father's Dogs." An earlier version of "The Honor and Glory of Hunting II—Clyde" appeared in *Sporting Classics* as "When the Walls Fell Down." Finally portions of the introduction appeared in *Big Sky Journal* in my essay "Hunting among the Indians." I am grateful to James Babb and Russ Lumpkin of *Gray's Sporting Journal* and Chuck Wechsler of *Sporting Classics* for publishing my work. I also acknowledge the influence of various friends on my work and on my evolving understanding of the woods: my old friend and colleague Wilson Hall; my camping buddy and the fisherman I hope to be someday, Mark DeSommes; my oldest friend and first colleague, Rodney Allen. I also acknowledge my wife, Ansley, for her support.

Introduction

On a windy, frigid morning when I was around ten, my father took me squirrel hunting for the first time. We saw nothing. So to keep the morning from being a total waste, my father taught me to shoot his old scratched-up, single-shot .16 gauge shotgun.

There was an old chimney standing on the edge of the wooded area where we hunted, the lone remnant of an abandoned, dilapidated tenant farmhouse. My father took some of the crumbling mortar from the chinks in the bricks and drew concentric circles on the chimney, explaining to me about load and wad and spread. Then he handed me the gun and told me to put the bead on the innermost circle and pull the trigger.

All these years later I still remember the roar of the gun, the jolt of the stock as it slammed into my shoulder, and the cloud of dust that burst from the bricks. My father took his pocketknife and picked the shot out of the bricks, forever imprinting on my mind the pattern of the pellets.

Two years later, when I killed my first squirrel with that same gun, I felt as if I had completed the process that began on that cold morning. I had connected to something deep inside me that had no name, a connection that only blood could allow. The time in which human beings have lived among twelve-lane freeways and tall buildings, buying their meat packaged in Styrofoam and cellophane from the supermarket, is a blink of the eye compared to the eons in which man hunted to survive. Little wonder the first shedding of blood is so memorable: it allows for a connection to the collective memory embedded in our DNA. It reminds us that eating comes with a cost—the life of an animal, the stalking skills of a hunter, venturing forth into the woods on a cold morning when mist covers the valley.

Because I grew up in the small-town South, I was never far away from the woods. The backyards in my neighborhood ended in weeded lots that led to fields and trees and finally wooded lands. The farmers who owned this land didn't much care if boys wandered the woods. They often didn't care if we hunted there so long as we were careful to stay away from buildings or livestock. What I didn't know was where the woods ended.

I suspect I thought that they never did end, that the farther you wandered into the woods, the more mysterious they became. I read stories about hermits who lived in the woods, about mountain men who had their fill of civilization and just wandered away to live wild off the bounty of the land. When schoolwork became boring or I had arguments with my parents or my brothers, I would imagine striking out with nothing but my shotgun, a sleeping bag, and some matches to start a new life, living among the tall trees the way I imagined people had lived before anyone owned the land. I had never killed anything other than a squirrel, and though I had been taught to clean squirrels, I doubt that I could have figured out how to cook one over an open fire.

As I grew older, I learned more about the woods, and I left behind notions of hermits and mountain men. Still, with each new animal I stumbled upon in my wanderings, the woods became more mysterious. I distinctly remember the first deer I saw.

It was a gray, windless day in early November. The trees were beginning to lose their autumn color, and brown and yellow leaves were everywhere—on the ground, scattered along tree branches, floating in the water of the creek at the bottom of a huge hollow where I walked. I didn't have a gun—I was just walking the autumn woods, scouting out places to hunt. I topped the hill just up from the hollow and came upon the remnants of a road—two trails in the leaves, following the crest of the hill. And there before me was a buck. He stood sideways in the road, looking back my way. He was so still that he seemed for a moment to fade into the brown world around him, but the grayish tint of the winter fur along his flanks stood out.

I didn't know to count the points on his antlers. All I knew was that he was the biggest wild animal I had ever seen. When he snorted and lowered his head, I thought he might charge me. Instead he ran, slowly at first and then picking up speed so suddenly that he seemed to vanish, almost as if the woods had opened and taken him back into the patchwork of leaves and branches and underbrush around him.

I walked to where he'd been, looked at the sharp marks his hooves had made in the dirt when he started to run. I would have never called him beautiful or majestic or any of those stale words that people use to describe the wild. I just knew that the woods were now deeper and more mysterious because he was there. There was life here that I could not fathom, could not know. Later, when I first saw mallards fly into a swamp lake or heard a covey of quail thunder into the air all around me, I felt much the same way.

At some point around the time I began hunting and exploring the woods on my own, I was also initiated into the stories that hunters told. They came from everywhere, gifts to all of us who hunted. Stories of uncles and grandfathers and friends and mere acquaintances and their encounters with the woods, with the cold, or with the dark, or with the wiliest rabbit anybody ever heard of or the largest buck that had ever breathed air and that incidentally had gotten away and was still out there haunting the woods—somewhere, somehow. These were stories told around campfires late at night after a day in the woods and a few stiff snorts of bourbon, or before sunrise and before the hunt over coffee and grits and bacon and eggs in local meat-and-three restaurants where all the waitresses wore puffed hair and tight jeans and were saints to put up with men who called them "honey," or "sweetie," or "beautiful," and weren't terribly generous with their tips either.

For me at least, the stories became a part of what kept me coming back to the woods because they reminded me that I never truly knew what was out there. The woods were a world in which the mystery of creation was forever unfolding, merging somehow with my imagination of that world, so that even when the story was a leg puller, I never knew where the truth ended and the exaggeration and out-and-out lying started.

The town I knew. The woods I would never know in any complete way. There were parts of the woods that no one had seen, that no one could know or own. That mystery, that sense of something bigger and older than man, something that man could not explain or own in any real sense of that word, was part of the draw and part of the storytelling. It was also what finally led me to Cherokee hunting stories.

Long before white men came to these shores, Native Americans hunted these woods, living lives in which hunting was a way of life, as familiar and necessary as breathing. Perhaps they knew the animals much more intimately than later hunters would. Perhaps they understood the relationship of hunter and hunted as a spiritual matter, not an issue of how big or how many. I often think that the ghosts of these early hunters still haunt our woods.

Two Cherokee hunting stories came to capture for me the mystery of the woods as I saw and experienced them as I grew up. They come back to me now when I wander in the woods. The first, "Ganadi, the Great Hunter and the Wild Boy," has been told by Freeman Owle and appears in Barbara Duncan's book *Living Stories of the Cherokee* (1998), a volume well worth the time of anyone wishing to understand the history of the outdoors in the South. It is an old, old story. Earlier versions of the story appear in James Mooney's *Myths of the Cherokee,* which was first published in 1900.

In Owle's version Ganadi is the village hunter, supplying a bountiful supply of fresh game for the village. But one day as he prepares a deer carcass, a single drop of blood falls into the creek by which he cleans the deer. This drop of blood spawns a mysterious, wild boy, who becomes a playmate of Ganadi's son. The two boys eventually follow Ganadi into the woods and discover his secret. Each day when he goes to hunt, he makes his arrows and bows from natural material; then he rolls a rock away from the mouth of a cave and releases one animal, which he kills with his bow and arrow. After killing the animal, he prepares its meat for the village to eat.

The wild boy talks Ganadi's son into rolling the rock away from the cave and letting out all the animals. The animals depart—running, flying, crawling away, and scattering over the earth. The people in the village begin to starve until Ganadi's son learns to track and stalk the lost animals to keep the village in meat. Owle ties the story he tells to the fall of man in the book of Genesis from the Old Testament: man must go back to the woods to find what he needs, to discover the connection that he lost. In this sense the woods are the garden from which man was expelled to wander, searching for a way back home.

In his *Myths of the Cherokee* (1900), still one of the standard reference books on its subject, James Mooney recounted a similar Cherokee story of origin. The animals gather to discuss what to do about man. He continues to expand the land he occupies, thereby decreasing their habitat. "This was bad enough, but to make it worse Man invented bows, knives, blowguns, spears, and hooks, and began to slaughter the larger animals, birds, and fishes for their flesh or their skins." The animals finally decide that they should give man a disease in retaliation for his encroaching on their territory, for killing and maiming them. Thus rheumatism is born, making infected men and women helpless cripples. The plants that man finds in the woods enable him to treat the disease he has acquired from the curse placed upon him. But the deer tribe ultimately agrees that its members will infect only those human beings who do not value the animals they kill. To those hunters who show respect and gratitude for the animals they kill, for the world itself, the animals will impart no diseases.

The hunter who respects the natural world knows the animal he kills, matches wits with it, understands the animal's sagacity, its beauty. In so doing, the hunter demonstrates gratitude, not just for the sport of hunting, but for the life of the earth itself. The hunter experiences the mystery of the woods, where life comes and goes without funerals or ceremonies, where one creature dies so that another may eat. The hunter goes into the woods early in the morning to enact one of the oldest rituals we as a species know.

The stories I have written and compiled here concern people who hunt. They are set in the South of the past eighty years among a set of fictional characters who are related by blood and/or locality. Most of the stories are set in and around the fictional small town of Sledge in the Piedmont region of South Carolina. Most of the characters are members of either the White family or the Chapman family. The families are united by the marriage of Jacob White and Rachel Chapman just after World War II, a marriage that produces one son, Jacob, Jr., before both parents are killed in an automobile wreck.

Some of the stories are linked not only by characters but also by events. A series of events that begins in one story will continue into another story or be referred to by characters in another story. Sometimes these people tell their own stories in their own voices. In such cases the name of the storyteller appears just below the title of the story. Other stories are narrated in third person. But aside from the two families—the Whites and the Chapmans—the unifying element in all the stories is hunting and a concern with the "lost woods." For the reader who is interested in more information on the genealogy of the White and Chapman families, I have included an appendix detailing family connections and histories. But for that reader who does not want to bother with genealogy, the stories stand alone.

Some of the people in these stories are noble, and some of them are not, for as the Cherokee stories recounted above demonstrate, hunting, like everything else that man does, is inextricably intertwined with both the nobility and the depravity of human beings, intertwined with life itself. As the story of Ganadi implies, we are "no longer in the land." Perhaps we must go back again and again—not only to find, track, and stalk animals to feed ourselves but also to try and find the lost woods so that we may remember who and what we are.

The Deer Hunt

1936

Jacob White and his grandfather sat on the hillside at the edge of the farm, near the point where the grandfather's land merged with the eastern edge of the Appalachian Mountains. Behind them the mountains were silhouetted in the sinking sun. It was a clear November evening, and soon the trees would be bare, their skeletal arms outlined against the mountainside and the horizon. But on this evening, they could still see splashes of brown and even orange and yellow among the straggler leaves that still clung to the oak and hickory and poplar trees.

Jacob and his grandfather were not looking at the leaves or the trees or the sinking sun. They were watching the valley below them, intent on the stream that ran along the edge of the farm. They knew that deer would come to the stream for water sometime before dark, and they were there to watch them.

The grandfather had taught Jacob to watch, had taught him the silence and stillness of watching so that you merged with what was around you, became one with trees and leaves and sky, so that for a time there would be only what you saw. And then, said the grandfather, you could know the earth, the place where you lived. Only then were you a hunter.

And that's why they were there, to hunt. The family depended on venison to make it through the winter, and the larder was emptying out.

They had no gun with them. It was back at their camp farther up the mountain. They merely sat there among the trees on the hillside to see the deer, so that the grandfather could understand what the deer were doing, where they were going, where they would be. The boy was dressed in a brown wool shirt and grayish corduroy pants. The grandfather wore his usual clothes: bib overalls and an old brown coat, a simple wide-brimmed hat. Both of them wore work shoes, often called "brogans" by the townspeople they knew.

The grandfather heard the deer before the boy did—heard them inside the sound of the wind that was blowing. He knew that soon they would emerge from the copse of oak trees that grew beside the creek.

And there they were: several doe—one trailing a spindly-legged fawn. They came into the open from the trees, stopping to look around them. Their grey-brown winter fur blended with the buff color of the sage grass that grew along the creek so that they seemed to merge into the landscape even as they stood there. And then one by one they went to the stream to drink. Before they drank, they stood still and looked around them. Sometimes their skin quivered or their ears twitched as they looked around.

After they had drunk and wandered back toward the woods, a large buck emerged from the copse of trees. He did as they had done, looking around him and then wandering down to the creek to drink. A few moments later he disappeared into the woods near where the other deer had vanished.

The boy and the grandfather headed back to their campsite. Along the way the grandfather stopped to examine several trees that had deer rubbings on them from earlier in the fall. He ran his hands along the bark in order to determine how fresh they were. He sniffed his fingers to see if he could smell sap. He also looked at tracks and scuff marks on the ground here and there.

And then he and the boy built a fire at their campsite. They said very little to one another as they ate and prepared for bed. They shared an easy companionship, born of many nights in the woods. Talk was not necessary.

The next morning farther up the hill, the boy watched his grandfather wait on the buck he had selected, the buck he would harvest. Somehow, the boy never understood exactly how, the grandfather seemed to know where that deer would appear. After they had waited for more than an hour in absolute silence, the deer appeared just up from the creek. The boy thought that it was the same buck they had seen the evening before, but he could not be sure. The buck was huge, with a large rack of antlers and a muscled chest. He grazed on the sage grass, raising his head to chew and look around him.

The grandfather steadied the 1894 Winchester against his cheek, standing perfectly still with the right side of his body leaning against a large hickory tree. He collected himself as he aimed the gun. Then he pulled the trigger.

The shot broke the silence as it echoed across the valley, and as it did, the deer looked up, turning his head toward them. He stood very still, quivering ever so slightly. A moment later he crumpled and fell. The bullet had pierced his heart. He was dead when Jacob and his grandfather got to him.

As he always did, the grandfather sat beside the deer and said a prayer of thanks to God and to the spirit of the deer. The grandfather was part Cherokee, and this was something he had learned from those who had taught him to hunt. He had taught the ritual to his son and to his grandson.

Then together the boy and the grandfather skinned and gutted the deer, quartered the meat and packed it on the mule the boy fetched from the campsite. The grandfather left the stomach, liver, intestines, heart, hooves, and lungs for the ravens, vultures, and other scavengers to eat. He placed the head and the skin in a copse of trees, sprinkling tobacco at the mouth of the deer to make his journey to the spirit world pleasant. Back at the campsite they packed the camping gear on the mule and headed back to the farmhouse where Jacob and his family and the grandfather lived.

Three years later the grandfather died, leaving Jacob White to remember this evening and many more like it. But two years after that, the memories had begun to fade amid the complications of Jacob's life. Jacob still hunted now and again, but his father had never been much of a hunter—what the grandfather had taught Jacob about hunting had never stuck with the father. The father had lost much of what he had learned from the grandfather amid the mad rush to survive the last decade.

The family did not depend on venison the way it once did. His father had gotten some cows and was having a mighty hard time making money off them, so they were eating more and more beef as a way of at least breaking even on the expense of raising them.

Away from the family and the farm, everyone was talking of the Nazis and the war that was raging in Europe. Jacob and his sisters heard it all the time at school. They saw it in the newspapers and discussed it at dinner.

"Can America stand by and let this happen?" one stark headline read.

But mostly Jacob's complications were personal. He was trying to finagle time with Rachel Chapman while working with his father at his maternal grandfather's hardware store and taking classes—one at a time—at Furman University, where Rachel was a sophomore and a full-time student.

Jacob's parents did not have the money to send him "off to college." His father thought he should stay home and make something of the farm.

"Don't waste what little we have on school. Take this land and make it into something I never could. Cotton's coming back. Gotta come back eventually. Besides, the land—it's all you got."

Jacob knew about the land, knew the stories so well that he didn't even listen when his father told them, stories of the grandfather who had taken him hunting. How the grandfather—"half to three-quarters Cherokee" his father would always emphasize—had sharecropped and bought the land acre by acre, eventually turning it into a sizable spread, where he grew cotton and corn and raised sheep and cattle. How he married "an all-white woman" and raised his family.

"And he had to fight for everything—'cause a his blood and all. 'Cause of the way he looked. Dark skin. Dark hair. But it never stopped him. Brought up three of us—taught us all to work. And he sharecropped, buying his land acre by acre. Always did what he had to do to put food on the table. Fought till he owned the land free and clear and didn't work for nobody but himself."

Jacob would watch his father stare out at the mountains west of where he and the grandfather had hunted deer. He could smell the bourbon his father'd been drinking—his late afternoon one or two or three, soon to become four or five—even six some nights. And he could see the bitterness in his eyes.

His father was not bitter about the hardscrabble childhood he had endured. He was bitter because he had not been able to keep the farm going. Cotton prices had fallen in the twenties, and then there was the boll weevil. And just about the time everybody thought the price of cotton would come back, the stock market crashed, and everybody was broke. And the Piedmont land his grandfather accumulated proved to be hard to work, especially during drought after drought. Because of all the cotton that had been grown there, people said it was not as fertile as the land closer to the coast.

Everybody was waiting, waiting for cotton to come back, waiting for a good year with lots of rain, but it never seemed to come, so now the farm was still there, and his father piddled at it—a kitchen garden, the cows he had lost money on, chickens—but mostly he had had to work in town at his father-in-law's hardware store. A store hardly big enough to support one family—let alone two. He had not sold any land—not yet anyway. But he was too broke to farm. "Too broke to live," he sometimes said after he had started drinking.

But Jacob's mother—turned gray and man hard by the endless struggle to make ends meet—would have none of Jacob farming. She was bitter about his father's failure. "The boy needs an education," she said. "He needs to leave the farm."

So Jacob worked in the hardware store and took a class a semester, his mother using her egg money to pay his tuition. And sometimes he wondered about the two sides of the grandfather. The near mythic man who had built the farm from scratch. And the other man who taught Jacob to know the woods, to hunt.

Then the big complication came and wiped away all the others: December 7, 1941.

Everything that Jacob had known or planned or thought or done was instantly a memory, existing in the looming shadow of war.

His father had never seen war, had never even ventured beyond that small region of South Carolina in which he had been raised. The mountains where Jacob and the grandfather had hunted were the boundary of everything the father knew. The same was true for Jacob's mother and for everyone Jacob knew.

So Jacob was cast back again on the memories of the half to three-quarters Cherokee grandfather. He who had died when Jacob was fourteen and had taught Jacob all that he knew about the woods, about hunting. He who had struggled and fought for the land that now languished in Jacob's father's keeping. He who had fought in World War I when he was a young man. Jacob wondered what the grandfather would say about his oldest grandson fighting to defend his country. What advice he would have. But the grandfather was dead, gone.

By February Jacob knew the date he would ship out. Rachel had agreed to wait on him, and he spent as much time as he could with her. But they both knew that all the waiting in the world could not ensure their future. Jacob was walking off into the unknown, and he might never come back. These last days together might be it—all the time they would have reduced to two weeks. They fought to hold onto each other, moving quickly beyond the kind of high school petting that had been the boundary of their relationship into a new kind of intimacy that scared them both. But they could not seem to stop themselves.

Still, for all that, the sex did nothing to quell the fear Jacob had begun to feel as the days continued to slide by one after one after one. He counted them and felt a kind of dark foreboding that he could not name, a kind of terror. But he told no one—he was ashamed.

And that was when he got down his grandfather's Winchester model 1894 .30–30 and hatched the plan that he would go into the woods alone for just one of those final nights he had before he left for war. He never had any clear notion of why he was going back to the woods. He just knew to go.

He took the rifle—which had not been fired in two years—two cartridges, a can of Van Camp's pork and beans, a spoon, a knife with a can opener built into it, a canteen of water, and the tattered tent and bedroll he had used when he camped with his grandfather.

He made his camp on a knoll just at the edge of the mountains in one of the places where he and the grandfather had camped. He even found one of their old eroded fire pits. It was mid-February—no time for camping in the foothills of the Appalachian Mountains—and the afternoon sky was the color of slate with dense gray clouds piling in from the West. The temperature dropped fast, and the wind blew as he set up the tent and arranged his bedroll inside it.

Then he built the fire the way his grandfather had taught him—neat, spare, conical so that the flames shot straight up against the darkening evening sky. At first the fire was loud with cracks and pops, but then the coals began to glow, and the roar was soft, and he was able to open the can of beans and heat it at the edge of the fire. Outside the circle of warmth from the fire, the air was frigid. Jacob felt the cold against his back. He pulled his hat low and moved closer to the fire.

He had not eaten all day, had been too preoccupied and nervous about leaving to want food. The thought of food nauseated him. In the days before that, he had eaten only when he began to feel the weakness in his knees or dizziness when he walked fast or climbed stairs. So he savored the beans and the rich sauce, spoonful by spoonful, as he looked back at the farmland, holding the still-warm can in his gloved hand and watching the darkness take the valley. He wished that he had brought two cans, three. He was hungry in a way that he had not been hungry since he had known of the war. And then he remembered the hunting trips with the grandfather.

He would have probably never seen the deer had he not stood up to get more wood from the pile of branches he had placed near the old fire pit. It was a buck, and he stood on the hillside staring off into the valley. The sun was almost lost among the winter clouds so that the deer was just barely visible.

Jacob stood still when he saw him, and the image became clearer as his eyes began filling in what the darkness would not let him see—the antlers, the chest, even the eyes that glinted in the firelight. He realized then that it was a buck, one almost as big as the buck that he and his grandfather had killed on that morning all those years before.

Jacob had not come to the woods to hunt—but the season was still in. The rifle was inside the tent, already loaded—more for protection than anything else. As he crept toward the tent and the rifle, he kept his eye on the deer, not really sure what he would do with the gun. But he looked away as he reached for the gun, and when he looked back, the deer was gone—his flight as silent as the night itself.

That night there was no moon, and the thick winter clouds cloaked the stars. The sky and the hillside were dark, as dark as the inside of a cave. Jacob tossed and turned in his bedroll, awaking again and again, shivering because of the fifteen-degree iron cold all around him. But sometime in the night, Jacob dreamed of the grandfather. For days, weeks, he had been thinking of war, of going far away from the only world he had ever known, from Rachel, and he had been longing for the presence of his grandfather, the calm abiding presence of that man who knew the woods, who had built a farm from nothing, who had known and survived war.

Now he dreamed that his grandfather took him into the mountains, farther into the mountains than they had ever been, and that he showed him the secret life that the animals lived there. The life there was very simple, so simple that Jacob had forgotten to notice it. The grandfather also told him what happened to him in the war. When Jacob woke up, he could not remember any of the secrets that had been revealed to him— they were all a blur.

He sat up abruptly. Pulled his coat around him, for the air was frigid. Snugged his hat on his head. Then he stumbled out of the tent into the cold.

The snow had come and covered the ground. There was a light dusting of it that had stayed on the tent. And then when Jacob began gathering wood for the fire, he saw the hoof prints all around the campsite. They were large and they disappeared up the hill into the mountains. Deer had been there in his camp during the night. One set of hoof prints was larger than any of the others.

Jacob built a fire to warm himself. He had no food for breakfast, but he was hungry just as he had been the night before after he finished the pork and beans. He sat close to the fire and watched the sun rise over the farmland that his grandfather had bought and farmed acre by acre, over the land where they had hunted. The storm clouds and the snow were gone. The sun was rising in a clear, cold sky. After a time, he packed his camping gear and hiked back to the farm.

Two days later, Jacob went off to Europe to fight. He did not know if he would return. But when he left, he took with him something of his grandfather and the land where they hunted. He left behind him his father, his mother, his sisters, and Rachel. She carried in her womb the child she and Jacob had conceived.

Stalking Glory

1956

The first time his Uncle Ted took him to the camp, the boy heard about the turkey. Because he was new to hunting and because there had been no man around his grandmother's house to tell him hunting stories, he could only listen and wonder.

The men were standing around the frame, a huge structure made of twelve-by-twelve cedar beams. Two of the beams were cemented in the ground, and a third was mortised into the tops of the other two. There was a crude pulley system set up on the crossbeam for hoisting the deer carcass and a concrete pad underneath that could be washed off.

But this November evening, the deer were all cleaned, and the whole area had been washed down. The men stood smoking and talking, looking off into the sunset, enjoying the last moments of a cold autumn dusk. In a few moments, they would go inside the lodge to eat some fresh venison in front of a roaring fire.

The boy would remember two things: the bone-numbing cold in the waning sun and the image of the old gobbler, with a nine-inch beard and inch-and-a-half spurs—too smart for any man to kill.

His Uncle Ted was leaning against one of the cedar beams, sucking down the last bit of his fifth Budweiser. "Hear that, Boy? Can't nobody call that old gobbler up. He's too damn smart."

His uncle looked over the boy's head, then turned and spit. "Have to go in and get that one on the roost," he murmured. "Shit," he said with a bit more volume, "I've seen the old cuss a million times in that old field behind your grandma's. I shoulda shot him then. Then yall'd all be talking 'bout me now."

It was the only time Uncle Ted had ever taken him hunting, and judging from number of times his grandmother had asked his uncle to take him before he finally did, the boy could expect to wait a while before he got to go again.

So at night after his grandmother went to bed, he would get down his father's old double-barrel, and open and close the breech just to hear that solid sound of steel on steel as it clicked shut, and then he would go to bed, wondering about that old turkey gobbler, so smart that no one seemed to be able to stalk him.

And then when early spring came, the boy was hit with the wild notion that he would be the one who would bring that turkey home. He, Jacob White, Jr.—only child of Jacob, Sr., and Rachel White, both killed in an automobile crash in 1946, when he was three years old—would bring that turkey home.

He had never before tried to fool his grandmother. He was keenly aware of the sacrifices that she made for him. Not because she reminded him, but because he appreciated how close he was to homeless. He had no parents. His father had made it through a world war, had come home to a son who had been born while he was in combat. But then he and the boy's mother had been killed together in an automobile wreck. Of this the boy was reminded whenever there was a school play or baseball practice or a family reunion or Father's or Mother's Day. Still, no matter what the old woman did for him, she could never be his father or mother. So he spent time trying to imagine the unimaginable: what life would have been like had his parents not taken that ill-fated trip.

There were no *World Book* encyclopedias at home. He read them at school that spring, learning all they could tell him about the habits of wild turkeys. He learned that turkeys fed in flocks, that they ate what they could find—seeds, insects, even snails. Feeding times were in midmorning and midafternoon; mating season was spring; and they roosted in trees—big trees, oak trees. Hunters, the writer pointed out, often stalked turkeys before they shot them. Sometimes they called them up with turkey calls.

As light lasted longer during the spring afternoons, the boy began haunting the woods behind his grandmother's house after school. It was a remarkable time in his life even before he ran into the flock of turkeys about a mile south of his grandmother's porch. He had been to the woods many times, but he had never really noticed the explosion of spring up close. That spring he did.

The woods began to change in late March. One day he noticed the buds protruding from the branches. Two days later, young leaves, startlingly green and soft and tender as baby's skin, shot forth up and down the branches. And then when the wild dogwoods flowered, he imagined that he saw snow. He remembered his grandmother telling him of the snow that came right before his father went off to war. She saw it as an omen that he would come back to her when the war was done. He did. Then a year and five months later, he had died in an automobile crash.

But when the boy found the flock, the turkeys were onto him before he even got close enough to look for the old gobbler. Indeed in 1956 wild habitat had not been encroached upon as much as it would be later in the century. Wild turkeys were wary of human kind. Only the stealthiest woodsmen got close to them. Still, for the boy one look was enough.

Every day he haunted the woods, stumbling upon the flock here and there, usually along the same ridge that led into the hollow of large, old oaks. He knew he had found them when they flew and skittered away. But slowly, by trial and error, he stalked them, not even knowing what he was doing. He upset them as many times as not, but eventually he matched his movements to the sounds of the woods, the blowing of the wind and the creaking of the trees, even the movements of birds. He matched the colors of his clothes to the color of the woods. Only after weeks did he discover their habits and pick out the one among them that he pegged for the old gobbler. He was not close enough to judge the length of the beard or the spurs, but by simple logic he determined that if the old gobbler were among them, he was that bird.

And then he encountered the big problem: getting the gun out of the house without his grandmother discovering what he was doing. Beside this problem, the woods and the turkeys seemed like minor issues.

His grandmother quite literally never left the house except when she took him to church twice on Sunday and once on Wednesday evening. She was home all the time because she was old and because she was there to take care of him, to get him what he needed and to be sure he was, in her words, "raised right."

And then fate stepped in: Aunt Rebba had her gall bladder removed, and after much discussion back and forth between this relative and that, it was decided that his grandmother must spend at least one night there with Aunt Rebba right after she got home. The boy hoped that his grandmother would consent for him to be left alone—after all he was twelve, soon to be thirteen. But no, she would have none of it. Uncle Ted would be brought in to stay with him.

Uncle Ted was by far the most derelict of all of his relations. The boy had never been sure how Ted was his uncle. He knew he was not his father's brother or his mother's brother. He thought maybe he was a cousin that he called "uncle." Black sheep of any family he happened to be a part of, he spent most of his time doing exactly what he wanted to do, whatever that might be at the time. That is why it took him so long to take the boy to the hunting camp. Most of the time, he was drinking beer and frequenting places that the boy's grandmother called in a hushed voice "honky-tonks." The boy was certain that Uncle Ted was his grandmother's last resort as a babysitter and that her thinking was that for one night Uncle Ted would be able to keep the house safe and free from fire or theft or corruption until she could get back home and raise the boy right.

Uncle Ted arrived just after the boy got home from school. He had a pasteboard box with fried chicken and cornbread in it, a six-pack of beer, and a change of clothes. The boy and his uncle ate the chicken and cornbread and watched his grandmother's black-and-white television: *This is Your Life, I Love Lucy,* and *Tennessee Ernie Ford.* Neither of them said more than a half-dozen sentences the whole evening. By the time the boy went upstairs to go to bed, Uncle Ted was working on his third or fourth beer. And the boy was thinking, *There is no way he will be awake enough to hear me creep out of the house at four.*

But the boy didn't count on the spring thunderstorm. He heard it rumble, gathering strength all night as he slept in the off-and-on fashion of one who plans to get up early for something important. By morning the rain was coming down hard, and he had a decision to make.

He reasoned it out. Given his grandmother's watchful eye and her early rising, this would be his only chance to get out the house with the gun with no one knowing. He had to go despite the rain. So he put on the clothes he had laid out the night before. He got the gun and the shells from where he had hidden them. The hard part was finding the huge poncho that had belonged to his grandfather. It was in the closet downstairs near where Uncle Ted slept, snoring softly.

Somehow it all worked. Just as he had planned, he stood on the porch in the dark, the gun in the crook of his arm and the shells stuffed into his bulging pockets. He headed out in the darkness, feeling the raindrops hitting the poncho like hail. Because he had spent so much time that spring in the woods, he knew how to get to where the turkeys would be by watching the tops of the trees along the horizon as the lightning flashed. Within thirty to forty minutes of his departure, he stood looking into the hollow of oak trees that he had reasoned would be the roosting place of the flock.

Picking the particular tree in the darkness and in the midst of a thunderstorm was something that he had not counted on. He stared into the dark treetops, the tree branches dark veins silhouetted against the sky when the lightning flashed. But when there was no lightning, he could just barely separate branches from sky.

He walked along the trees, hoping for a miracle of some sort. The *World Book* encyclopedias were of no help now, nor would any of the lore of turkey hunters have been of any use had he known any of it. He was at one of those points in the life of every hunter where success depends on some strange combination of luck and human reasoning. Only one fact worked in his favor. The constant dribble of the rain and the occasional rolling roar of the thunder made it easy for him to cover the sound of his walking. Still he did not know if he were within twenty yards of the turkeys or a mile. And suddenly it seemed that there were more trees than he remembered and that their branches went on forever, up and down and around the sky.

And then the strange thing happened. He looked up at just the right moment, and as the lightning flashed, he saw something on the limbs of an enormous oak tree twenty or thirty yards away that was not of the tree. The birds seemed way too big for the tree, like dinosaur birds in a prehistoric forest. But after patiently waiting for the lightning to illuminate them again, he knew that he had found what he came for.

He stood still for at least five minutes, waiting for the trembling to go away so that he could move into position without attracting their attention. Then he moved, slowly and carefully putting himself in what he thought would be good range. He made sure that he could kneel to shoot and that he could use the trunk of a tree to steady the gun.

He was in position when his hands started shaking again. So he waited some more. And then he realized that he had no way of knowing which bird was the old gobbler. He knew instinctively that he would have to depend on size and luck, and if he killed a hen, he killed a hen. So he compared sizes of the dark forms, putting his bead finally on the biggest and holding it there until his arm hurt. And then when the lightning flashed again, he steadied his aim and squeezed the trigger.

The gun sounded like the explosion that would end the world, fire escaping out the muzzle of the old shotgun like Armageddon's flames. There was a flapping of large wings and some rustling and then the sound of the rain again. His shoulder hurt where the gun kicked him.

He stood up, not knowing what to do. He did not know what you did after you killed your prey, especially if you did not know whether you had in fact killed it or not. So as he crept toward the tree, he looked carefully about him to see if an enormous bird, winged but not destroyed, sought revenge or lumbered off into the wet darkness.

He found the bird under the tree, almost stumbling upon the carcass before he saw it. He grabbed at the bird, discovering almost immediately that his aim had been true. With the luck that comes only to boys and dogs, he had killed the old gobbler instantly with a clean shot.

In the gray April dawn on his grandmother's porch, Uncle Ted scratched at his bare, hairy stomach and looked down at the gobbler.

"That beard ain't no nine inches and them spurs ain't hardly an inch, if they're that much. So I can't tell you if it's the one they was talking about." He paused to yawn, drawing his breath in with a harsh inhalation.

"But I tell you one goddamn thing," Uncle Ted continued. "That's one big bird for a boy who ain't never been turkey hunting. One goddamn big bird."

Together the two of them, the orphaned boy and the black sheep uncle, cleaned the turkey and prepared it for the grandmother to cook.

"Now when your grandma gets home," Uncle Ted warned. "You tell her I took you hunting this morning, you hear? She'll throw one more fit if she thinks you went out and killed this bird all by your lonesome. That part is just 'tween the two of us."

"Yes sir," the boy said.

The General

1958

This story was found among the papers left by Reverend George Thompson, a retired Methodist minister who died without heirs. He died in the early 1980s at seventy-two years of age after having been run out of his last church, when he was around sixty-two, because of a rumor that he was known to lick a cork here and there. A passionate hunter, he often enjoyed telling and composing tales about the strange relationship between animals and people in the woods. Some who heard these stories insisted that the rumor about the drinking was certainly true because he talked like no minister they knew and much of what he said was embellished beyond reason and might indeed have been the result of more than a little imbibing. Folks also said he was a better shot than any minister had time to be.

No one knows if the story is true or false, but there are several members of some of the older hunting clubs around Sledge, South Carolina, who insist that every word is gospel and that the Reverend Thompson never lied—at least when he was talking about hunting.

The Reverend Thompson's Narrative

Everybody had heard of the General, but few had hunted with him since he was a puppy. His owner, Reverend Eddie Chapman, had taken to fundamentalism in a hard way. The other Chapman boys in town—his cousins and nephews mostly or at least people who went by the name

Chapman—were far from fundamentalism or even church as far as that goes. In fact rumor had it that a number of them were out and out alcoholics who frequented all manner of honky-tonks and had never shadowed the door of a church—mostly because on Sundays they were waking up with a hangover in the arms of one or another of a group of disreputable women.

Some folks said it was because Rachel Chapman White, Eddie's aunt, was killed with her husband, Jacob White, in that wreck just outside of Sledge in the 1940s. A tragic event it was—they left behind them a son, who was raised by old Mrs. White. And this after Mrs. White had raised her own children and after old man White had succumbed to a heart attack when he was in his midfifties. It seems like some folks are just born unlucky.

Well, folks said, the Chapman boys had turned to drinking because they had tragedy in their family. But I sort of dispute all of that. Yeah they did a little bit of drinking, but not all of them. Now Carl, Eddie's brother, was bad to drink sometimes. Still, he took care of his family. And you know how folks will talk in a small town. And then there was so many Chapmans around that I was never sure how they were all related. Well, at any rate, old Eddie chose a different path. He took to God. But it was not the broad path to the Lord—it was the narrow one.

Folks said that religion turned Reverend Chapman ornery and mean, that he spent hours and hours poring over scripture and thinking about sin. And then he started meeting for breakfast at Doug's, the local meat and three, with other hardcore ministers of the faith, those who spent hours and hours drinking coffee and talking about the deplorable state of the world and listing those who were directly responsible for it and would as a result feel God's wrath.

And it was somewhere about then that he became very picky about the people he hunted with. They had to be redeemed to his satisfaction. And to ensure this fact, he required that they reveal their salvation story to him sitting on the porch before they went hunting with him. The beagles would be howling and whining in the dog boxes in the bed to the truck, so as to make it more urgent that the teller of the salvation story get the story right, for only if they were truly redeemed would they get to go hunting. In this way the General became an agent of the Lord—at least according to what folks say about the Reverend Chapman.

Some folks said all of this was because Reverend Chapman's family had so many deadbeats in it, so that he decided that he had to set the record straight. Had to prove that once he found the Lord, he would do better than your average believer, even your average preacher. He would not just shun sin—he would also shun sinners. "If your eyes sin, why pluck it out," the good book says. Or something like that.

Well, it was a shame because by now the General was getting on to be about three, and he had established quite a reputation in Yellow Bluff and Sledge. All the hunters knew who he was and had heard stories about him. And now that he was taken out of general circulation for a number of years, there was no real way for anyone to verify any of what was told about the General and his rabbit-hunting prowess.

The other problem was the land itself. Old Eddie Chapman had inherited about half of the big old Chapman farm down near the river, and he had more or less let the place go to pieces as he pursued one hair-brain notion and another until he threw his lot in with the Lord. And now he was so concerned with preaching and sin and hell that he had no real time for farming. Well you can do no better for the rabbit population than let the farm go to rack and ruin. The fields became overgrown with ground cover that gave the rabbits something to eat and places to burrow and hide. And with the river on just the other side of the hollow at the edge of the farm, there was plenty of fertile soil around from where the river has flooded over the years. So the ground cover grew and grew.

Now I don't mean that old Reverend Chapman gave up on farming all together. Sometimes he'd plant a field or two of corn or cane, and he kept a few cows and some chickens—almost like he wanted to keep up appearances. But it was never his main preoccupation. And people knew that nobody had really made a living of that farm in years. So the rabbits and the rabbit hunts in that region became—well damn near epic. Especially if you threw the General in the mix.

And it was stories like that that caused Richard Haas, a newcomer from Alabama, to set out to find out about the General and about the farm. He was determined to prove that the General either was or wasn't the best rabbit dog in the world. Indeed he was determined to prove that the General existed, for there were those (still are far as that goes) who swore that all you heard about him was mere talk. Exaggeration. And Haas was also determined to see some of those fat rabbits that Chapman's farm was famous for. And if he had to get religion to do it, well so be it.

And of course that was what was required. So Richard started working up his salvation story. He tried it out on a number of ministers to be sure it was just right, and they gave him pointers. But most of them pointed out that, given what they had heard about Reverend Chapman, he might want to throw some more fire and brimstone into the mix. So Richard worked some more on it. And then he worked on delivery. It had to be fast, so as not to delay the hunting. And it had to be dramatic, the way most salvation stories are. It never does if the person saved was always a pretty good person. It's much more impressive if the person is a scoundrel. As one preacher friend of mine said, "You have to be saved from something, so it had better be something that's worth being saved from." Well Haas developed a past that would have even scorched the reputation of a politician or even a lawyer.

Now in order to understand the rest of the story, you must understand the various ways in which rabbit hunting affects hunters.

For most rabbit hunters, it's just the hunt itself same as with other kinds of hunting. There is something in the blood that causes all of us hunters to feel excited when we go out into the world to nab meat for ourselves. It's how we live—how we've always lived. But modern times have driven us indoors to dwell among televisions and lawyers and church committees and frozen foods and annual reports and such. Little wonder that when we become an active part of that process, we feel alive again.

But for others there's more at stake. They become so involved with the matter of getting the rabbit because they are on the side of the beagle. And they are usually on the side of the beagle because they resemble the beagle—I mean they're short and pudgy with stumpy legs and they're tired of people outrunning them, outmaneuvering them. Such was the case with Reverend Eddie Chapman. He had a gut that spilled over and flattened out his belt, and he had likely spent his life envying tall, lanky men in the same way that the beagle envies setters and pointers. So rabbit hunting was a bit like evening things out, making sure that life is fair. He likely thought that God Almighty had given him the General in order to compensate for his portly, stumpy body. And tell the truth, Haas was heading in that direction himself. He was a little bit taller than Chapman, but he was built low and squat like fire hydrant—a thick man. And already, though he was a young man and right spry at that, he was already developing the telltale gut that was beginning to crowd his belt.

Well, when Haas had perfected his salvation story and disappeared into that backcountry out from Sledge and near the river where the Reverend Chapman sat every day poring over scripture, the boys all sat around at Doug's speculating on what would happen. Would he come back with marvelous tales of cottontails and beagles? Or would he slink back into town having found out that his salvation story was lacking and that the only glimpse he had had of the General was through the door of the dog crate in the back of Chapman's Ford F150? Or would he say that there was no General at all?

At this point, the narrative shifts, and Reverend Thompson begins telling the story in the very words of Haas. No one knows if this is because Haas never existed and the Reverend is telling the story about himself or if he was simply trying to intensify the effect of the story on a hearer or if Haas actually wrote the story down for Reverend Thompson. Working only on Sundays, preachers have lots of time for mischief. That means that they can hunt five to six days a week if they want. And it means that they spend a considerable amount of time perfecting tale telling. Go to church if you don't believe me. I'm as devout as the next person—I go every Sunday. But I have never yet sat through more than two or three sermons in the same church without hearing a stretcher or two.

The General

Haas's Story

I thought when I got there that the problem would be the salvation story, but that was not the case. The Reverend walked onto the porch with his double-barrel .20 in his hand and his field outfit on—why he looked primed and ready to go. He leans his gun against the wall there, pulls his pants up over his stomach, and then extends his hand.

"So you the boy wants to hunt with the Gen'ral?"

I nod my head.

"Well, let's go," he says, nodding his head in the direction of the truck where I could already hear the beagles beginning to yap and bellow and whine.

Well I had spent so much time working up that salvation story that I was not about to just forget about it.

"Reverend Chapman," I say. "I thought you'd wanna hear about—"

"Oh, yeah, yeah, yeah," he says, "I do like to know about who hunts on my land, with my dogs."

So I start in telling it. But along about a quarter of the way through, he grabs my arm and says, "You sound all right to me, boy. Let's do some huntin'."

Well within about ten minutes, we're bouncing through fallow fields and over old dirt roads until we get down in that land that borders the river. He's talking a blue streak about this and that: politics, the government, his worthless brothers and cousins, the importance of tithing, the sins of Hollywood, the divine nature of the Ford F150. "There ain't no truck like it nowhere."

Then all of a sudden, we pull up in a little short gap in the trees along a dirt road and stop with a jolt that damn near sends me through the windshield. The river is somewhere over to the right, and to the left is a long beautiful hollow with a creek running through it that eventually empties into the river and briar and bush patches here and there. And on the other side of that is a field that is pretty much grown up with weeds and scrub timber. It's rabbit country sure nuf.

The General looked nothing like I'd thought he might look. In fact, even after the Reverend pointed him out to me, I had trouble distinguishing him from the other hounds. Chapman directs the dogs down in the hollow, and they begin to sniff out the area around the creek, getting into some of those cut banks where there are hiding places. Well suddenly the dogs are onto something. It's then that I understood why they call him the General.

He's the dog that makes the announcement and heads up the troops. And if any dog gets in his space, he growls in this low, mean voice like he means to give one warning and one warning only.

"Grhhhhhhhhhhhh," he says. Then he sucks in a little air—making this "ugh" sound—before you hear it again, a little louder and more ragged: "Grhhhhhhhhh." He's the lead dog and the other dogs had just better stand back and let him set the pace. Well, the other dogs are true believers. They just give him room and look away, showing the whites of their eyes and tucking their tales and slinking away as if they don't even want to think about what might happen if they get him all riled up.

Then when they hit pay dirt, the sound of his voice is like a bugle call, only no bugle I've ever heard has anything like outrage and joy in it all at the same time. And this dog's voice does. So the call is to alert everyone to the situation. He has found the villain, the offender—indeed he has found the prize. And everybody had better just fall in line because the chase is on, and he's the General, leading the chase.

Chapman and I are standing up the hill from where the chase starts and the rabbit darts right out in front of us close enough for a shot, but the Reverend just watches, sort of shaking his head as if to say, "Whoa and don't he run though."

At first I think he's crazy or slow, and then I realize that he just wants to enjoy the chase, take his time, listen to the sound of the dogs. After we listen for a moment or two to the music of six or seven beagles on the trail yapping and bellowing, Chapman casts his head to the side and closes his eyes.

"Hear that?" he says, shaking his head from side to side. "That high-pitched kind of wail 'bout a pitch or two above everyone else?"

I nod.

"Well, there he is—that there's the Gen'ral."

He looks around at me, shifting his gun to his left hand so he can use his right to pull up his sagging pants. "Ain't he sompthin'?" he says. "The Lord made only the one. That's all." He holds up a chubby finger.

Chapman knows just about where the rabbit'll reappear, so he puts me up the hill a ways, and he takes the low area down close to the creek. We hear the wails and the bellows get soft and then they get a bit louder back over our shoulders as the rabbit does his circle and begins to head back to home turf. Then the Reverend takes that little double-barrel .20 of his and sights down it just to be sure all is right with it.

Then here comes the rabbit. I am unsure of the etiquette, but I figure since I'm the guest, I get the first shot since the rabbit is coming about midway between us, but before I can even aim, I have moved around too much and the rabbit has seen me, swerves and heads more in the direction of the Reverend. I hear the pop of the .20 gauge, and the rabbit does a flip and falls dead between us. And then the dogs—here they are piling in all in an uproar 'cause of the shot.

The General is clearly in the lead, and he's clearly the retriever. He's on that rabbit in snapping-finger time, shaking him here and there a bit before the Reverend says just as if he's talking to a person, "Now Gen'ral, that's just about enough."

At that the General drops the rabbit and stands there panting with the other dogs. The Reverend holds the rabbit up for the other dogs to sniff and examine. He's a well-fed bunny—ain't no doubt about it. But we aren't there to play or to congratulate ourselves. The Reverend gives the order, and the General and the other dogs are at it again.

After we bag two more rabbits in just about the manner we bagged that first one—me killing one and the Reverend one more—the General strikes an enormous cane cutter. By now we're closer to the river, hunting in the Johnson grass along the far edge of a fallow field that's separated from the river by a thin line of sweet gums and cane in a swampy bit of land. That old rabbit comes out of the grass kicking up dirt with his big old back legs, and you can hear in the General's voice a note of near panic.

It's as if they have just now started the real hunting—those first three were just for grins. He's found the rabbit that set the world off balance.

"I be dog," the Reverend says. "Don't see that many a them, particular ones that big." Then he lets go of a chortle. "Boy, we in for a tussle. That there's a thoroughbred."

This is the first time in the hunt that I have seen the Reverend strategize. Part of the problem is the Johnson grass and cane that grow in that swampy land along the river. "That rabbit get in there," says the Reverend, "you won't be able to smoke him out. And them dogs get all hung up in the mud. Might lose the scent."

He shakes his head and looks at the sky. Then he just listens to wailing of the beagles for a minute or two. Thinking.

"All right," he says finally. "There's just one thing to do here."

He places me on one edge of the swampland and he goes up and gets down in the grass itself. He seems to think that the rabbit'll seek the grass.

It's a while before the rabbit comes around, and he's leading the dogs on quite a chase, but the Reverend's positioning of us works perfectly. It prevents the rabbit from getting in the thick grass and disappearing. But the damn rabbit is so fast that he just smokes by us like a runaway train from hell before anybody gets a shot.

And then by the second circuit, I can tell that the dogs'll soon be getting tired. They've already run down three rabbits, and this big old swamp rabbit looks as if he still has a marathon or two in him. Like he's just enjoying the hell out of this. Like he was born to it. The dogs are having a mighty hard time keeping up with him. So when I hear him coming a third time, I hatch a plan of my own. I decide I'll move him toward the river and box him in.

And then the unexpected.

Apparently the rabbit has done a switch back to fool the dogs, but it doesn't work. And when they round the bend ahead of me, the General is about twenty feet behind him and the other dogs about ten to fifteen yards back from the General. The General's barking and yapping has become one continuous, anguished yawp as he pushes his short legs as fast as they'll go so he can get closer and closer to his quarry.

And then the unexpected again. The damn rabbit disappears.

Now I know he didn't really disappear, but what I'm telling you is this. I'm looking right at him coming along and he turns or jumps or gyrates so fast that I don't see where he goes.

Well there's mass confusion among the dogs 'cause they don't see where he's gone either, and they're dead tired to boot and can't seem to follow the scent. And it's then that I notice that the General has gone. I assume he's still chasing the rabbit, but for some reason that I will never know, he's silent. Maybe he didn't want the other dogs horning in on his prize rabbit or maybe he's just as stumped as they are, but with his reputation and all, he has more on the line than they do.

Without their leader, the other dogs splinter and wander off in several directions, panting heavily. But they come back pretty quick because they don't seem to find anything. I look up at the Reverend and shrug my shoulders. He does the same back to me. We scan the woods and cane and the Johnson grass, but it's as if both dog and rabbit have been transported by damn magic out of the vicinity.

The silence probably lasts only about five minutes, but on a rabbit hunt in the midst of a chase with a dog like the General, that's a damn long time. Eerie too. The silence I mean.

Then from out of nowhere I see something coming through that damn Johnson grass between me and the Reverend. It's real hard to see, but the dry seedpods on the top of the grass go to trembling. And suddenly it's as if the General has been restored to life on the spot by God Almighty. His wailing begins in midwail and the sound seems to go into the stratosphere, hitting notes that I bet the General nor any other beagle has never hit before. And here they're both coming right at me, 'cause the rabbit has seen the Reverend in the Johnson grass.

"There he is," screams the Reverend.

I break the rules a bit and step directly in front of the rabbit and draw a bead on him, but the damn General is so close, I'm afraid to shoot. So I move toward the river, which causes the rabbit to move even closer to the river.

Well unbeknownst to me, the Reverend has come up behind me even closer to the river, so that when the rabbit seeks to return to the canebrake and Johnson grass, he's got the Reverend to contend with. And then the rabbit does something I have never seen a rabbit do before. He disappears again, switching around here and there. And the next thing I know, he's heading for the river. And then he soars off into the river like some sort of winged creature out of a damn dream.

No, I wouldn't have believed it if I hadn't seen it with my own eyes. But I ain't lying or even exaggerating. It happened. And he hits the water like a water spaniel. And I can still see him such a remarkable sight it was. That head bobbing in the water, those ears plastered back as if in a pompadour, and him swimming like a damn otter.

And then I see the General jump in after him—only he don't look nearly so spry as that old rabbit. He hits the water with a loud splash almost like a rock. And there the two of them are swimming the damn river right at the swift part.

"Goddamn," I hear the Reverend say behind me, reverting back to the language of his honky-tonk past. "Goddamn," he says again, louder this time.

By now the other dogs have hit the shoreline and are bunching up and yelping and howling like a bunch of banshees. They pace the shore and whine, but nobody is willing to enter the water. I guess that's why he's the General and they're not.

For the second time I draw a bead on that damn canebrake rascal, but just before I pull the trigger, I feel the Reverend's hand on my arm.

"Uh-uh," he mutters right in my ear, "Ain't no way to retrieve him. We only kill what we eat on this farm. It's the Lord's way."

Well, by the time the rabbit makes it to the other side and skedaddles up the bank and shakes himself good, he's just as fresh as if the race has just this second started. And the General's a quarter mile downstream caught in the current. There's been lots of rain and the river is high and fast. Suddenly I see that the General is struggling, and then I see his head bob a couple of times.

"He'll come up," the Reverend says—all confident-like. "Just give him a minute. No rabbit can beat him, not even a canebrake varmint like that 'en." But I see on his face that he's worried.

And then when we still don't see the General break the surface of the water, we head downstream to look for him. But though we search up shore and down, we do not find the General. Though we stay late into the night, building a signal fire for him and calling his name again and again, though the Reverend prays to the Lord, the General does not come. The water of that old river is not to release him.

At this point the narrative comes to abrupt end. But the story goes on as they say. Reverend Chapman never did get over losing the General. Some folks said he gave up on religion in his despair at losing his prize beagle, but I dispute that fact. I still see him in a church now and again. What he did give up on was preaching and that sort of hard and mean fundamentalism he had adopted. I suppose he felt that a God who could create such a remarkable dog as the General and then cut him off in his prime because of one spry swamp rabbit was more than he could understand, let alone explain to other folks. And of course the same God created that canebrake rascal, just as he created you and me. It's just too much to understand. Too much for a feeble human brain to deal with.

It was in some small way just like the death of his Aunt Rachel—just one of those things that you can think about until you die, but you won't find any real explanation. You just have to have faith.

So Eddie Chapman still believed, mind you, but rather than assuming that he knew the ins and outs of God's plan and who was in God's favor and not, he assumed that the Lord works in mysterious ways—which is what I've always thought. The only thing that we know for sure is that he loves all his creatures, including beagles and rabbits and even canebrake rabbits and short-legged fat men.

So Eddie Chapman went back to farming and restored the farm to some order, which of course cut down on the rabbit population. Then he got married and had a couple of kids and started raising chickens. And yes, there were no more of the epic rabbit hunts of old. But in his own way, I guess the General was an agent of the Lord, for he brought the Reverend Chapman back to a proper view of God and creation. Kept him from being hard and mean in his religion. Kept him from hating folks. Kept him from being bitter.

But for all that, the General still lives in the hearts and minds of rabbit hunters around Sledge and Yellow Bluff. Folks tell stories about him actually catching and killing rabbits himself without hunters to help. Some even say that he came out of the water some miles down the river and started a new life on a new farm and sired a whole generation of beagles who could outdo any swamp rabbit in the world. And they say that if you listen real hard on autumn nights when the cold comes in and just begins to make folks shiver and think about going hunting, you can just barely hear his high-pitched yelping and barking as he chases down yet another spry canebrake rabbit.

But as inspiring as all of that is and as much as I'd like to believe it, none of it is true. The truth is what I have set down here with the help of Reverend Thompson and Richard Haas from Alabama. The General drowned while chasing a swamp rabbit in 1958, and if Richard Haas is to be believed, he was the best damn rabbit dog that has ever been or ever will be. Yes. Why yes indeed, God made only the one.

Slick's Conversion

1961

"Couple hundred acres of prime Piedmont South Carolina land over there in or near Laurens County," Slick is saying in his ragged, incredulous voice. "Excellent quail country. Ex-ceee-llent. Up and bought it—paid cash. What I hear."

Though there are five men in the barbershop, including the one in the chair, no one comments.

Slick takes a quick drag off his filterless Camel and continues as he lets the smoke drift out his mouth and nose: "Goodly portion of it had been the old Ramsey place. Old man Ramsey lost ever'thing trying to keep a farm going in the 1920s and just flat give up and took to the bottle. The family held onto the land somehow, not really doing much a anything with it as children moved away, went off to other parts of the country. And then one day somebody decided that it might be a good idea to sell it and put the money to use. So this here Ivor up and buys it. Everybody thinking he's going to farm it, but he don't. He hunts it. That's right. Hunts it."

Slick's talk gives the impression of hurry—as if he expects someone to shut him up, so he's got no time to get his tone or emphasis just right. He's just got to get the words out fast as he can.

It's a small shop—a one-chair, one-barber enterprise, smelling of hair pomade, shaving cream, cigarette smoke, and old, stale newspapers. But the regular customers don't much notice the smell. They sit in the line of metal and vinyl chairs that face Samson's chair, waiting their turn to be

36

trimmed, and talking quietly, so that sometimes their voices sound almost like water gurgling in a stream as the long, quiet, small-town afternoon ticks away in little bits and pieces. But when Slick's there, he does most all the talking, so the others just listen. And the sound is more like that of rushing water, pushing obstructions out of the way.

But no matter who's there, most everyone is more interested in the talk than in the haircutting, some of them even staying around after they've been trimmed and paid. Slick has so little hair left that he could easily cut his own—thus the name "Slick" describing his shining bald pate. But every two weeks, sometimes every week, he comes in for a haircut and a shave, holding forth except when his face is covered with shaving cream and Samson is applying the straight edge to his cheeks.

Samson Matthews, the barber, is slow and methodical in his work. Commenting just enough to keep the conversation moving, he never takes a firm position on any matter of politics or local gossip—though he does take delight in goading the big talkers like Slick. But every evening when he goes home to his portly wife, Olive, he tells her everything that he's heard. And she spends a portion of the next day telling all her friends what he told her. So everything discussed at Sam's acquires life, walking about the little town of Sledge—even if the real people in question have little or nothing to do with the stories they inspire.

On this resplendent, late October day, Slick is talking about a man very few people in town have ever laid eyes on. They've all participated in the endless speculation that his arrival in town has inspired. He's a newcomer—not from around there—and though he reputedly is related to the Chapman clan in some distant way, nobody knows how or even if this is true. And since he reputedly bought a large track of land just outside of town and no one has been formally introduced to him, an enormous suspicion has possessed the tiny town. It's as if they all think that he should have introduced himself to everyone, declared his intentions in buying the land, even asked permission before buying it. Now that they know he paid cash for the land, their suspicion seems justified. None of them can imagine an honest man with that kind of money to throw around.

"Well, he rents some of the land, Slick," Samson the barber interjects. "I know that for a fact. He's a retired professor from Virginia."

"Yeah, rents some of it out to farmers who grow cotton," Slick says, picking up the sentence Samson has thrown out, so as not to be upstaged or shut up. "Rents some of it for pastureland. But most of it just sits so this here Ivor and his black boy can hunt on it, train their dogs on it."

"A professor with that kind of money?" Steve Johnson interjects. "Don't make no sense. Family money?"

Ignoring Johnson, Slick looks at Samson in what might be a challenging way if Samson were paying attention to him. Then he continues, "Yes suh. That's a fact. Trains his bird dogs on the land, dogs he loves better than he does his wife, some folks say. Him and the Negra. What I hear."

For a moment or two, the only sound is the snip-snip-snip of Samson's scissors and the slow thunk, thunk, thunk, thunk of the ancient, unbalanced, two-blade ceiling fan that stirs the stale air above everyone's head. Samson keeps the fan going pretty much year round, for with a crowd in the barbershop, some of them smoking, the air inside is stuffy no matter what the temperature outside.

Slick crushes his cigarette out in an ashtray on a table strewn with a disorderly heap of magazines—primarily *Field and Stream* and *Life* and *Time*—and old copies of the Spartanburg newspaper, then looks around the shop. "Well, he ain't asked me to come out there to hunt no quail. Ast any a you?"

A few of the men shake their heads no and grunt a short laugh or two. But no one says anything. Slick is the undisputed best bird hunter in Sledge, and he is well known for the pointers that he keeps in a small pen in the backyard of his ranch-style house. He lets them out only when he hunts them, which is just about every Saturday during quail season, and twice a summer when he forces each one of them into a vat of gray/white-colored liquid he calls "flea dope."

"Them rolling hills, those longleaf pine savannahs on the south side. Perfect for quail. Long as you don't take the farming too seriously," puts in a tall, gaunt man named Melvin.

"Well, he don't take nothing but bird dogs seriously," Slick says. "That's a sure thing." He shakes his head. "What I hear."

He's quiet for a moment, letting the dust of the conversation settle before he erupts again.

"Ain't asked me neither," he says again. "And that land just a settin' there the whole time the Ramseys owned it posted against hunting. Prime quail country. Prime. And now there's a fellow owns it and hunts it, but he ain't asked me out. Still got the posted signs up."

Slick is known about town for hunting quail just about anywhere he can, even occasionally wandering onto posted land or even into people's yards. In part this is because he owns no land of his own except the small lot his house occupies. Still he has permission to hunt on various farms in the county. But he is by nature a wide-ranging hunter in the same way that a setter is a wide-ranging bird dog. So if he knows there are quail in an area, he has a hard time staying away—even if the land is posted or otherwise in use. And if he doesn't know there are quail in an area, he has a hard time not wandering on the land to investigate the possibility. Quail hunting and fishing are his passions, the weekly reprieve from working ten-hour days as a foreman in the sawmill twenty miles from town.

Once in his ramblings, his dogs pointed a covey in the cemetery that adjoins the property around the Sledge Baptist Church while a wedding was going on. Slick saw all the cars and was trying to call his pointers off. But when one of them locked down and pointed a mere fifty feet from the church and the other backed him, he later told the minister that he had no choice.

"Couldn't hardly help it. Them birds flushed. Be bad for the dogs to have them point and me do nothing about it."

He killed two, one with each barrel.

Inside the church, a pair of shotgun blasts punctuated the wedding vows, causing both bride and groom and a number of the attendants to visibly flinch. When people found out Slick was hunting near the church, nobody thought much about it.

"Sure 'nough shotgun wedding," the father of the bride said to the minister.

By now Samson has finished his customer, collected his money, and tipped his head to Slick. "Your turn, mister. Let's go. We ain't got all day."

Slick stands up, still talking.

"But this here's the funny part: he don't much like to shoot quail. I tell y'all that part? He just likes to train the dogs and work the dogs and watch 'em work, so that's why he invites other people out to do the shooting. Can you beat that? And he ain't never asked me out."

Now as he approaches the barber's chair, he turns and faces the line of vinyl and metal chairs and stands there for a moment like an orator or a preacher even.

"And here's the part really gets me. Got this black fella who practically lives with him and the wife. And he's like the best bird-dog trainer in the world, according to what this here Ivor tells folks. I tell y'all that?" He shakes his head back and forth.

"'Magine that—black boy training bird dogs. And sometimes his—the Negra—brings his friends out to hunt. 'Magine that."

"Have you ever seen the man?" Samson asks, shaking the apron out as Slick settles into the barber chair. He has a smirk on his face, though no one notices it, certainly not Slick.

"Who?"

"This Ivor you call him."

"Can't say that I have," Slick says, shaking his head. "No, not that I recollect any rate," Slick shakes his bald head again as if he has never really thought about that side of the issue.

"Well you sho' talk lots for a man ain't never laid eyes on a fella," Samson says as he tucks the apron around Slick's chin.

But everyone else is now thinking about the race issue. It has divided the country of late what with the sit-ins and freedom riders and Dr. Martin Luther King and nonviolent protests of one type or another all over the newspapers, all of which have been discussed in some detail in the barbershop. But no one in town has personally witnessed or been involved in any of these events. In their little town, life just keeps its slow pace. Day following day following day and on and on and on.

The black people live their lives, and the white people live theirs—separate but equal according to the way the white folks view the matter. But that they have an example of the races mixing in new ways right close to town—well folks would need to think that out. And then the money—nobody they know pays cash for a farm. Yes, folks would need to think and talk to get all of this straight. There's something strange about a man with that kind of money.

And then as Slick adjusts himself in the barber chair, there occurs one of those strange, inexplicable moments of coincidence that sometimes change the shape of the earth and the people on it in obscure and incalculable ways, even in small out-of-the-way places such as Sledge, where nothing ever happens.

Ivor Wilson opens the door to the barbershop. He stands there with his setter Alice.

Most of the men don't know what has happened. And though Slick figures it out in just a moment, it's only Samson who has met Ivor.

Most of the men watch the dog. In their experience, no one has ever brought a dog of any kind into the barbershop, so they steal glances at Sam to see what he'll do. But Sam does nothing.

"Mind if I bring ole Alice in here wi' me?" Ivor Wilson says, looking at Samson. He's a tall man dressed in clothes just a bit too nice for a day in town to get a haircut: a tweed coat, a plaid oxford shirt, and one of those little Tyrolean hats perched sideways on his head with quail feathers stuck in the band. His hair is shaggy and unkempt, the grayish-white color of it telling them all that he will not see fifty again.

"Naw," says Samson. "Bring her on in here."

Samson has already tipped Slick back in the chair and begun lathering his face as the fan continues its rhythmic thunk, thunk, thunk, thunk.

Alice the setter sniffs the air for a moment or two, then follows Ivor Wilson to his chair. He tells her to stay, and she lies down on the tile floor in front him, looking around the place for moment or two. She twitches her nose and moves her head back and forth, picking up the strange pomade-laden smell of the place. Then she puts her chin on her paws and prepares to go to sleep.

Resplendently white and ticked with orange and black, she's the sort of dog that appears in paintings of bird hunters in the field. An English setter of the Llewellyn line, she is brushed and washed, giving the appearance of being as much a pet or even a show dog as a hunting dog.

For a few moments, no one says a word. And then Ivor Wilson says in an upper-crust Virginia drawl, "Hope you boys don't mind Alice. She goes most everywhere I do."

A chorus of "naws" and "course nots" from the gallery of sitters.

Despite his lateral position in the barber chair, Slick strains his eyes and turns his head to watch Ivor Wilson as Samson strops the straight razor.

Melvin Rogers pipes up, more to fill the silence than anything else. "So what's the secret ah training a good bird dog like that one there, mister? And I assume you do hunt her."

"I do hunt her. Yes indeed." Ivor Wilson says. "And trainin', well, it's sorta like this. First don't assume that you know what she's thinking, 'cause you don't. She ain't a human being. She's a dog. And I don't mean that the way you think I do." He looks around the room and stretches his legs out a bit.

"When I say she ain't a human being, I'm saying she's different. Doesn't see the world the way you do. The world doesn't look the same or smell the same or sound the same or taste the same to her as it does to you. And what that means is you gotta respect her. Now that doesn't mean you let her run you over and rule the roost 'cause ever creature that God created wants to be the boss of something or other, and it's finding out who can boss in one area and who can boss in another that makes things work the way they're supposed to work. Especially with bird dogs."

Nobody expected such a lengthy answer, but Ivor Wilson is a talker, and he's just getting going. Most of the men had been looking forward to a few moments of silence after Slick's incessant chatter—they know that he can't talk with Samson applying the straight razor to his cheek. Time to think, to reflect on what's been said, particularly the race matter. But now—since it appears that another talker has taken the floor—well that would have to wait.

"So you teach her how you want her to communicate with you, and you decide where y'all are going to hunt. And then she teaches you what it's all about. She takes you huntin'. 'Cause she understands the birds. Knows what they smell like, what they taste like raw, what strange, glorious creatures they are 'cause she's pretty damn strange too, come to think of it. She is the strangeness that you have forgotten about and left behind after you became civilized and started going to school and church and eating with a fork. And she takes you back to that some kind of way."

Now Ivor Wilson pauses and looks around the shop.

"Boys," Samson says, as he cleans his straight razor with a small, damp towel lying across his shoulder, "this here's Ivor Wilson. Bought the old Ramsey place out from town."

"Pleased to meet you boys," Ivor says.

Everybody is now contemplating the fact that Samson has been holding out on them, that he never let on that he knew this Ivor Wilson the whole time that Slick was holding forth. But Samson is not thinking about them. He's just relishing the fact that he has shown Slick up, and Slick has been silenced by the straight razor he is applying to his cheeks.

"You the one—" Slick starts up, but Samson bears down on the other cheek with the straight razor, and he won't let Slick finish his sentence.

"So you just quail hunt?" Melvin says just to forestall the awkward silence that threatens again to fall over the shop as the men sitting there resist the urge to gawk at the man everyone has wondered about and talked about for all these weeks.

"Yes sir," Ivor says. Ivor adjusts his long legs and wiggles a bit to get his hips comfortable on the vinyl seat, and then he takes off again. "The bobwhite quail is the noblest of birds. He's got class. Now most a you men know about what the mother bird'll do to protect her young—why she'll pretend to be wounded. Just like a human being, she's willing to give her life for her children. No chicken'll do that. Well, the male will do the same. Not everybody knows that, but it's true. In fact, old Bob White will raise the young'ens by himself if he needs to. I mean sitting on the nest all the way to staying with the young til they're on their own. No rooster'll do that. Bob White—he's a gentleman."

Wilson pauses to look down the row of chairs at his listeners. "Most a these birds don't live much more'n a year, but they live well. So the hunter comes in and takes the extras at the beginning of the time of year that they start coveying up. But me, I don't too much like the hunting part. I like training and working with the dogs and then watching 'em work. Nothing in the world like it."

Ivor clears his throat and continues, and then as he talks on and on about quail and setters, it becomes clear to all there that this is a man who loves to talk even if no one is listening. Still he's new in town, and since he is the mystery they have all been discussing for lo these many weeks, nobody has the gumption to shut him up, so that by the time he pauses again some minutes later, most everyone has stopped listening but Slick. Several of them are even planning ways to get the conversation back to something that won't inspire a lecture.

Slick, still lateral in the barber chair, has been moving his feet from side to side for quite a while, and as soon as Samson wipes the final bit of shaving cream off his face and applies the aftershave, patting it softly on each cheek, he fairly leaps out of the chair.

"Mister," he interrupts, almost before his feet have hit the ground, "You might own some prime land and you might have some pretty dogs, but you don't know shit about bird dogs."

Slick extends his hand to Ivor Wilson in a challenging way and says, "Ed 'slick' Jones, quail hunter and dog trainer."

The contrast between Slick's peremptory explosion and Ivor Wilson's slow, long-winded musings is stark, causing most of the men sitting in the gallery there to straighten themselves and prepare for a scene. But Ivor Wilson seems not to register what has just happened—almost as if he missed the point of Slick's attack.

"How's that?" he says quietly, shaking Slick's hand without standing up. "Your name?"

"You can call me 'Slick.'"

"Pleased to make your acquaintance, sir."

Slick stands there in front of Ivor Wilson, still wearing the haircut apron, and delivers a lecture of his own.

"Well, first of all, you don't baby no huntin' dog. You take him huntin'— he don't take you. He ain't a pet. He's a hunter, and when he don't do what he's s'posed to do, you whack him good—let him be a example to the other dogs. I've known hunters let the dog sleep in their beds, play with their kids. But I ain't never seen no pet can hunt birds. I can show you a thing or two about bird dogs and about quail hunting. I might not know much, but I know bird dogs and I know bird hunting. Now where exactly's your place?"

Alice the setter has now raised her head and is watching Slick in a sleepy way. She changes her position, sprawling on her side, stretched across the floor so that her nose is nearly touching the toe of Slick's work boots.

"Well as far as the pet part goes," rejoins Ivor, "you're looking at a pet that can hunt birds. Ole Alice there's a fine dog. Best there is—won awards. And I certainly would allow her to sleep in my bed, but my wife, Molly, won't hear of it. She's very fastidious about dogs coming in the house. But pretty much everywhere else I go, she goes. And I'm still aworkin' to get her in the house."

There is still about Ivor Wilson the air of a man who does not recognize that he is being challenged, attacked even. The men in the gallery can't decide if it's simply dull-wittedness or some sort of refusal to be baited into a fight. In fact he is beginning to get that look on his face he had when he was extolling the virtues of the bobwhite quail, as if he might just tell them all in great detail about Molly too.

But there is no time for Ivor Wilson to talk about Molly, for a new look has come across Slick's face too, moving from bottom to top as a blush would, but this is more of an expression of excitement, as if he has remembered something so important that it will upend the conversation.

"Mister, who trains yo' dogs? I might be able to help you out. I'm serious now. I can help you if you let me."

"Well, I do sometimes. But my good friend Eric—why he's the brains of the outfit. He's my partner. We talkin' about opening a kennel, raising and breeding setters, doing some field-dog trials. Building a hunting lodge. The whole bit. We both love the dogs, and we love the sport."

"This the black boy I been hearing about?" Slick spits back.

"He's black, but he's not a boy. He's probably forty-five. Got a couple of kids. Doesn't need to work—his wife's from Chicago and inherited money. Bucoos a money. And I'm a retired college professor. We used to teach together. So we both decided to come south to quail country to do something for love rather than money. Went in on the venture together. He owns 80 percent of the land and me 20. I don't have his kind of resources."

Slick was all ready to move onto the issue of why a black dog trainer would not do, but now he's faced with a larger reality than that, one for which he has no words: the specter of a rich, landowning black man in this country of poor black and poor white people who are separate but equal according to the way most white people see the matter. And the black man in question is from Chicago—the North. He's a professor.

The rest of the men look to Slick to say something: to confront this new wrinkle in the issues they have all debated and thought about for lo these many slow-moving months. Not because they think he's smarter than they are, but because they know he's a talker and that he's always got something to say. That he'll say pretty much anything. That he'll say what they won't even think. They want him to, though often they will say later that Slick should have kept his mouth shut.

But he is silent. There's only the thunk, thunk, thunk, thunk, thunk, thunk of the fan.

"Well," Slick says finally, pulling a cigarette from his front pocket, "I gotta be heading home. Gladys wants me to drop in down to the store."

He turns and heads for the door, the unlit cigarette in his mouth. As he puts his hand on the knob, Samson says, "Hey Slick, you don't want no haircut?"

Slick looks down at the apron he still wears, remembering why he came in. He appears to be confused.

"Naw, naw. I best go." The unlit cigarette bobs in his mouth as he talks. He takes the apron off and hands it to Samson. "Put it on my tab."

But as he turns back to the door, Ivor Wilson calls after him.

"Come on out and go huntin' with me and Eric. Bring your dogs. We'll show you how it's done Virginia style." Ivor Wilson is smiling broadly.

Slick has his hand on the doorknob, has turned it so that the tumbler has pulled out of the latch. But now he pauses in midstride, still holding the doorknob, but not opening the door.

"I might just do that," he says, looking back at Ivor Wilson.

"Don't might just do it," Wilson says, still smiling. "Do it."

"Let me think on it," Slick says. Then he opens the door and leaves, shutting the door behind him with a thunk.

Olive Matthews is getting ready for bed, coating her face with a green cream that is supposed to make wrinkles vanish.

"So anything happen today I need to know about?"

Samson is propped up in bed reading the Spartanburg newspaper. He has on reading glasses and has been drinking a glass of buttermilk. There's still a little bit left in the glass that sits on the bedside table.

"Not really," he grunts.

"Find out any more that man bought all that land? That Ivor they call him."

"Found out he didn't buy much of it."

"Well, who did?"

"Black fellow name of Eric—from up North. Chicago. Rich man."

Olive stops applying the cream and looks at Samson.

"Black man?" she says. "He move down here? A rich black man from up North?"

"Yep."

"Well, I'll be. What folks gon' do?"

Samson puts the paper down and looks at her. "No, I'll be to it. There ain't nothing they can do. The world's a changin'."

"What Slick have to say about it?"

"Oh everything and finally nothing much of anything. Just like always. But you mark my word. You mark my word with chalk and underline it twice. He'll be huntin' with this Ivor and his partner Eric—the black man—fore it's all over. They'll all be best friends. 'Cause there's quail involved, prime quail land."

Olive looks back at the mirror and continues with the application.

"Yes indeed," he says with a look of satisfaction on his face. "Quail hunting will have done what Congress and presidents can't. Make people wanna work and live together."

By now Olive has finished her application and crawled in bed. Samson puts the paper down, takes his reading glasses off, and drinks the last bit of his buttermilk. Then he puts the glass on the bedside table and turns off the lamp beside the bed.

Samson turns on his side to go to sleep. Olive is lying beside him on her back. She is looking at the ceiling.

"Well, I'll be," she says. "What'll they think of next?"

The Honor and Glory
of Hunting I—Luke

1961

Johnny Chapman

My mother had three boys. My father used to say that we were as different as night, day, and then something that resembled neither night nor day. He never bothered to tell us which one of us was night and which was day and which one neither one, but I think I know. I was the middle one, and I was nothing like either one of my brothers or my father. I took after mother—quiet, shy, too patient for my own good. I was neither night nor day—just something nobody could explain.

My brother Larrie was a good bit older than me and wild as a damn buck, sort of like my daddy. He was a tough guy—played football, caroused with all of those high school toughs, always making sure that we all knew who was boss. Went off to Vietnam when I was still in my junior high school, came back madder than hell. And then there was Elvin, a good bit younger than me. He got out of Dodge pretty fast and moved to Alabama—down around Mobile. Still there. He don't visit or call very often.

We were all three hunters just like my father and a number of our other relatives, including Uncle Eddie, the preacher-farmer. I guess maybe it was in our blood. But given the difference in ages—we were all three at least seven or eight years apart—we wound up doing it pretty much on our own. Daddy was an excellent shot and a profoundly good bird hunter, but his patience had its limits. He'd take you out and show you how to shoot and all, but he was not interested in teaching you the marksmanship skills necessary to be a bird hunter. He didn't have enough patience for that. I guess he felt that you should learn that just the way he did: on your own.

So by the time I got my first gun, an old scratched-up, hand-me-down .410, Dad and Larrie were going bird hunting and leaving me at home because I was too young, made too much noise, couldn't hit the side of a barn—well you know how that goes. That just left me with nothing but the urge to go, so I started hunting squirrels near home. Though now I may look back on that as a kind of deprivation, particularly when I contrast it with the glossy pictures of deer, turkey, and even mountain-goat hunting that I see in sporting magazines, back then it never crossed my mind that I was deprived. Sure I would have preferred hunting with my father and brother, but I was and am a patient man. And if that could not be, well I would do my best with squirrel hunting. I found a number of friends around Sledge and Yellow Bluff who were in similar circumstances for one reason or another—one of them was my cousin Jacob. Their fathers were too busy to take them hunting or their fathers were dead or had left. So we would hunt together.

We would meet about 4:00 P.M., at just the point when the autumn sun in South Carolina was beginning to show the first signs of fading slowly into the horizon. I had my single-shot .410, and though as I recall Roy also had a .410 and Jacob a .16, neither gun was any more than a double-barrel if that. And the stocks of their guns, like mine, were scratched and pitted from riding in the back of cars and trucks without the protection of a case. They were old guns, passed down by fathers or uncles who either had gotten better guns or who had given up on hunting all together.

We met in the afternoons, because we knew (I'm not sure from where) that squirrels were only active early in the morning and late in the afternoon. Two or three blocks from home, where the road became dirt and somebody's farm started, there were two or three acres of woods that nobody had cleared and cultivated—who knows why. And there we would sit and wait.

We had no one's permission to hunt there because we figured that the landowner already knew that all of us boys hunted there, and if we were careful not to hit a cow or to shoot within a couple of blocks of a house, he would never say anything. Some of the land was probably family land, Chapman land. But I didn't know where it started and where it ended. And nobody really cared.

After all, who cared about the population of squirrels? Even back then in South Carolina, some people wouldn't eat them, called them "limb rats," and talked about their close family connections to the rat. And then there was the way they looked on the plate. No matter how you cooked it, a squirrel leg was still a squirrel leg, all flexed and ready to jump up at you.

But around Sledge and Yellow Bluff some people were poor enough so they needed to eat squirrel, and though my family didn't quite fall into that category, my father was southern enough and sportsman enough, so that he would not disdain a meal of squirrel, and he firmly believed that you should never kill what you did not eat. So if I hunted squirrel, we ate squirrel, and I ate it too, though I cannot say that I really liked it that much.

But I did like hunting them. I liked everything about it. I liked the way the sun sank in the autumn, slow and somber and still like the end of somebody's life. I liked the way the cold crept on you so that you didn't know you were going to be cold until you were already cold. I liked the crisp, solid sound of the breech of that single-shot .410 snapping shut. I liked the red color of the shell casing and the smell of gunpowder and the fire coming out of the end of the barrel that you could only see when the sky was almost dark.

I have often thought that something of human intelligence could be divined by watching the way a good squirrel hunter finds a squirrel that's hidden in a tree. You never look at a tree the same way after you squirrel hunt. Even a tree that has lost all its leaves is a puzzle for the man who knows that there is a squirrel hidden in it. And when red, brown, and yellow leaves are on it, you have a puzzle worthy of a keen mind.

I once found a squirrel hiding on a large branch no more than ten feet up the bole of an enormous oak tree. He was clamped against the tree in plain sight like a tumor of some sort, and I was standing a mere fifteen feet away. But though I knew the squirrel was in the tree, had seen him go there and not leave, I could not see him. I thought he was a knot. It was by process of elimination that I figured out where he was and shot him.

Later in my squirrel-hunting life, I would have never made that shot. It was unfair in that it gave the squirrel no chance to run and at such close range it ruined the meat even with my weak .410. But it did teach me that the squirrel, rat relative that he is, is a worthy opponent. Somewhere in his tiny brain that squirrel recognized not only how to hide but also the rather complicated notion that in a pinch hiding in plain sight would defy the hunter's expectation. I took from that experience a new respect for the intelligence of squirrels, and that made the hunting mean more.

It was that kind of thinking that caused all three of us to become disgusted with still-hunting. There was something dishonorable about it, we decided. It was like a soldier shooting the enemy at the dinner table or in the bathroom. Everything has to eat, and when you sit and wait for the squirrel to come out of his nest and forage, you give him no chance. Now we were boys, and our nobility had its limits, and I seriously doubt that we would have given up still-hunting for squirrels had it not been for my dog, Luke.

He had been around the house for a year or two, and nobody had thought much about him. I can't really remember where he came from or how we got him. I remember my mother saying that he would be the last dog we would take in for a while because the monthly budget was getting rather close. We fed him table scraps, but he had to go to the vet every year, and that set us back upwards of ten dollars, a damn fortune in that day. She would always say things like that, standing out there on the back porch giving us all the what-for like she had had it with every damn one us. But we knew when the next stray showed up, she would relent. She was a patient woman—else she could have never lived with my father or my brother Larrie. Even me every once and a while. But every now and again, she just needed to shout for a while before she went back to being patient again.

But no one would have called him a hunting dog of any sort. Hunting dogs were supposed to be hounds, or pointers, or setters, or spaniels, and he was none of those. He was many fathered, and if his mother wasn't a stray, then her owner had quietly dropped him and all his brothers and sisters off, figuring that they would be taken in or starve. He was black all over except for brown on his feet and chest, so I assume he had a bit of Manchester in him. But it must have been only a bit because he was smaller than most Manchesters and given to nervousness, like a Chihuahua. My father noticed him barking at squirrels and following them with his eyes along the tree limbs in our yard, and on a whim Dad got his bird gun and killed one. I guess old Luke had never realized there was a chance one could be caught and brought down to his level. After that he never forgot.

So my father says, "You boys ought to take that old Luke out to hunt squirrels with you."

Squirrel hunting was never the same again. At the sight of the gun, Luke was all business, and when he hit the woods, he was as serious as a surgeon exploring the inside of a diseased organ. We waited on the barking because we knew that if it reached a certain level of intensity, there was always a squirrel there. But we very quickly exhausted the three acres of woods that had been our haunt for all our hunting lives. Luke could scout out that area in no time flat, and though he usually found a squirrel or two, the commotion of his barking and running and our shooting meant that all the other squirrels stayed in hiding or took off. So, we expanded our range, leaving earlier and driving deeper into the woods on the other sides of pastures.

A larger area meant that the dog could range more. So we would stand and wait for him to bark. The sound was like lightning in our veins. I've heard the mournful sounds of coonhounds and the ragged bellow and yelp of beagles. Luke was like neither of these. There was something frenetic about the rhythm of his bark. The closer he was to the squirrel, the faster the bark went, and the range of his voice, from high to low, seemed at times almost human. We would run like hell to get to the tree, often

53

winding up in woods we had never seen, and usually when we got there, the squirrel was nowhere to be found. But this allowed us to understand the genius of the dog and to become better hunters.

I firmly believe to this day that he was never wrong. Yes, there were times that we could not find the squirrel. But we all believed that on those occasions we were simply outsmarted. And that is just how it should be with hunting. If you always get your prey, then the game is fixed, and skill and strategy mean nothing. So when we didn't find the squirrel, we began chalking one up for the other side and went on to another part of the woods.

Hunting with a dog gave us new feeling for the sport and made us feel like real hunters with the odds tipped in our favor as compared to still-hunting. It was only fair to give the squirrel a fighting chance, so we set some rules without really talking about it too much.

We all agreed we would not shoot directly at the squirrel until he ran. Even if we saw him hugging the tree thirty feet up, we would shoot below him so that he would have a chance to escape. This way we felt a bit nobler about the whole ordeal. And in the process, we all three became better shots. I was in the habit of just throwing up and shooting. If the squirrel was sitting still, a quick shot like that brought him down, but if he was moving, you had to keep your wits about you. That meant you had to steady yourself and carefully take aim, deciding how much to lead. You even had to notice how the squirrel ran, where he would pause, what he was likely to do next. I learned pretty quickly that the squirrel would always pause before jumping, so I would move my gun to the end of the branch and wait. Roy, by far the noblest of the three of us, noticed this and commented.

"You're doing nothing more than still-hunting."

"No," I said. "What if he don't stop, or what if he chooses another limb?"

Roy shook his head and spit. "They always stop. You got a damn shotgun, although it's a real weak one. By the time your pellets get up there, they're spread out the size of a softball. We not talking about any great skill."

I still didn't admit that I was wrong, but I was and I knew it. If I were going to be a true hunter, one who could become a bird hunter and go with my father and my brother, I would have to hit the squirrel running. This meant that I had to become even more focused—not easy with the excitement of the squirrel running and the dog barking. But I was determined to be a better hunter.

Still sometimes I wonder where that came from—that desire to become a better hunter. Seemed like we were infected with it. Perhaps we were just naturally drawn to excellence, but knowing my vast array of failures in my life, I have my doubts. I like to think that some of the dog's intensity rubbed off on us, for despite the fact that he was a dog and a rather pathetic one at that—coming from nowhere and having to beg his way into a family—his commitment to the sport was damn inspiring.

Luke never got bored or lost focus. He never did the dog equivalent of just throwing up and shooting. Luke watched us and watched the tree so that when he saw us aim, he was ready, and when the squirrel hit the ground, he was on him. I saw him come back with the squirrel clinging to his nose, ripping away at the delicate skin of the nostril or with the squirrel writhing in his mouth. He never let go. Luke would shake the squirrel from side to side, growling ferociously. But he was a realist. When it was over, it was over. He dropped the dead animal at the feet of the nearest hunter and was off to search for another animal.

Once I watched Luke chase a wounded squirrel into a hole that ran under a rotting stump. The hole didn't look very deep, but when Luke started rooting around in it, the dirt fell in a bit, and I realized that the hole was much deeper than the dog was long. Luke would stick his head into the hole and push forward; then he would come out snorting dirt and go back again, every time getting a little bit deeper until finally I realized he would soon be submerged, completely underground.

"That hole could cave in on him. The squirrel ain't worth losing the dog," Roy said. "Call him off."

So I tried, but there was no use. The squirrel was in the hole, and Luke wouldn't rest until he had him out. So I did the only logical thing. I grabbed Luke's tail, and immediately the dog plunged deeper than he had been before, so deep that my arm was pulled beneath the surface of the ground and I was prostrate over the hole.

And then I felt Luke pushing back toward me. I pulled, and out he scrambled, covered in damp, cold swamp dirt, snorting mud, and shaking the squirrel from side to side. He was nothing but intense, nothing in the world but intense.

But as I was to learn from squirrel hunting, real hunting is full of irony. It was the very intensity that Luke conveyed to us that ended our hunting bonanza. On a gray November day, Luke treed in a small oak tree out in the middle of nowhere. When we got to the spot, we all had our doubts. The tree was no more than twenty feet high, and absolutely bare except for a few leaves on the small branches right at the top. But the dog was absolutely convinced that a squirrel was in the tree. He barked in his high-pitched, by-damn-there's-a-squirrel-there voice, his eyes fixed on the top of the tree and glowing with conviction. We all three walked around the tree.

"Should we shoot up there and roust that sucker out?" Jacob said.

"Shoot at what?" I answered. "There ain't nothing there to shoot at. You can see every inch of that tree."

We walked around the tree again and again, and nothing moved.

Roy, ever the noble one, said quietly, "Shooting at this close a range is gonna blast whatever's there to smithereens. Either he's there or he ain't."

He ranged his eyes up the tree. "And I say he ain't." He turned to walk off. "Even if he is," he added over his shoulder, "this is no shot for anybody to make. We're too close, and the squirrel has no chance."

We followed Roy away from the tree, but the dog stayed, barking and moaning as if he would go crazy. We tried calling him off, with no success, so Jacob and I walked back to the tree. Roy turned to watch us, but he didn't go with us. He just stood there, half turned toward the small tree where Luke barked and half turned toward the surrounding woods.

And that's when the squirrel moved. In all the years that I squirrel hunted, I never saw a squirrel do what this one did. There was a rustle in the very top of the tree and then the small body of a squirrel comes arcing out into the gray November air, his tiny feet already grasping for the ground beneath him. He knew it was going to be one hell of a race, and he was getting ready for it.

Luke never missed a beat. He was after him. But all of us knew that the squirrel would win the race, so I guess that's why Jacob and I lost our wits and threw up and shot at ground level. I am thankful to this day that I was not the only one to shoot, for neither of us hit the squirrel, but somebody hit Luke. He flipped once and, like a shot rabbit, lay still.

When we got to the dog, we realized the orneriness of reality, for the dog was not dead at all, only paralyzed. In fact, from the looks of the wound, it was a fluke, a stray shot or two that had dropped below the wad and entered his spine. So we had to watch the dog that had led us on so many hunts try to figure out why his back legs wouldn't move.

We knew he would never hunt again, but in my guilt I thought that I at least should keep him alive and take care of him since I might have been the one to do this to him—even if I wasn't, I might as well have been. But then as I watched him drag his back legs around and pee all over himself, I realized that he would be better off going to sleep. As I made the decision, I thought that in a strange, ironic way, Luke was still teaching me. I was being a realist. When the squirrel is dead, there is nothing to do but go look for another. I would end Luke's misery, and then I would get another dog, I told myself. My mother and I took him to the veterinarian and put him down.

My father gave me the lecture that fathers give to sons at such times— *watch where you shoot, the one who shoots the gun is always responsible for what the lead that comes out of the gun does. This could have been a person you hit.* But these words were somehow rather insignificant. He didn't have to tell me that I was an idiot—I already knew that.

The real lessons came from the hunting itself. For as insignificant as squirrel hunting is in the larger order of hunting, it had become the place where I was to learn all that I would ever know about the rules of the game. Yes, the squirrel that Luke treed made two mistakes in strategy, two hysterical decisions that almost cost him his life. A squirrel always needs to be able to jump from tree to tree so that he can have several escape routes open to him. This squirrel had apparently been foraging out in an area without a network of trees and then, rather than taking his chances and attempting to outrun the dog on the ground, he chose the small tree that had precious few places to hide and that connected to no other tree. So, when we got to the tree, he was cornered, surrounded. But he had been lucky, and sometimes luck will pull you through. He got another chance at outrunning the dog, and he took it by jumping out of the tree.

Our mistake was more inexcusable, for we had not been under the pressure of being run down. We only had the excitement of the dog and the hunt to contend with. But we allowed it to tempt us into doing what we had taught ourselves not to do: shoot without thinking, without gathering ourselves to aim, without reckoning the cost. We were greedy. We wanted to kill the squirrel no matter what. And the price we paid was far too high. We lost the chance to hunt again.

Oh we tried to hunt squirrels again. I tried and tried to find another dog. But as far as I knew, you could not buy a squirrel dog in the way you could buy a setter or a pointer—even assuming I had the money, which I did not. You could only find one by chance hanging around somebody's house. And you only have the kind of luck we had had with Luke every hundred years or so. And we had grown beyond still-hunting. So as the next autumn approached, we looked forward to the prospect of giving up hunting all together or trying to talk my father into taking us bird hunting, something he declared we were too young for.

And then my mother stepped in. I guess she had seen me moping around the house for days on end. Or maybe she was afraid I would start being a homebody and get in her way.

So she's sitting there one evening reading hunting magazines. Go figure, I thought. And she sees this ad for mail-order squirrel dogs, thirty-five dollars plus shipping expenses. Well my mother was not a reader of *Field and Stream* or any other hunting magazine, so I knew she was looking for a way to help me out.

Mother showed me the ad and asked me what I thought. The ad proclaimed Cisco Kennels to be the best breeder of coonhounds and squirrel dogs in the country. It had a drawing of a dog of some sort howling at the bottom of a tree, his snout pointed skyward.

"Call us," the ad invited. "You'll probably hear the dogs howling in the background."

"Interesting," I said, handing her back the magazine. I couldn't imagine where such a kennel found its dogs or trained them. After all Luke had never been trained. We had merely relied upon his natural instinct. Nor could I imagine that my parents would spend thirty-five dollars plus shipping to get me a new squirrel dog.

Well it was close to my birthday, and my mother took the plunge without my knowledge or my father's.

Early one early Saturday morning in September, the phone rang. I answered since I was the only one up.

It was the local airport. They had a dog in a crate that had been shipped to us.

"A dog?"

"Yep," the voice on the other end says. "Comes from Cisco Kennels out in Arkansas. You gon' come get him?"

"Well, I guess."

"All right," said the voice on the other end. "The shipping expense is fifty-five dollars, payable by money order or check. You get to keep the shipping crate."

So I roused my parents, and after a brief intense discussion of the cost of the shipping—"Damn time and a half again as much as the stupid dog," my father said, still bleary eyed and sleepy—my mother and I got in the car and headed to the airport in Spartanburg.

The Honor and Glory
of Hunting II—Clyde

1962

Johnny Chapman

He was the color of a gun barrel and about two or three times bigger than Luke had been. He had some feist in him and a bit of something that my father would later identify as "mountain cur." He was solidly built with a broad chest and floppy ears like a hound dog. When I grabbed the crate at the airport, he snarled at me. So we got the airport shipping men to load him into the back of the truck, planning not to take him out of the crate until we got him home.

Given the growling plus the near one hundred dollars we had tied up in him, I was afraid to release him outside for fear that he would take off back to Arkansas, so I talked my mother into allowing me to open the crate in the house.

"Just so we can see what he'll do," I said.

So with several of us standing around to watch, I gingerly opened the door to the crate and stepped back, ready for him to come out fighting. But he didn't.

Instead he went to the nearest vertical object he could find—which happened to be a kitchen cabinet—and lifted his hind leg to pee.

"Oh shoot," my mother said. "Look at that. We should have known."

He peed and peed and peed in a strong, steady stream, the urine splashing off the cabinet and running along the edge of the linoleum floor and puddling in the corner. By the time he finished, my mother had opened the back door.

"Come on," she screamed. "Come outta here, you, you—!"

But he had other business to attend to. As soon as he finished urinating, he hunched up and took a crap on the kitchen floor.

By now, my father was in the room and in an uproar.

"Get that goddamn mutt outta here," he yelled.

Buying the dog was not his idea. For him the only kind of real hunting was bird hunting and deer hunting—one hundred dollars for a squirrel dog was insane.

There was talk of sending him back to Arkansas and getting our money back. I heard my parents fighting for days about it. But in the end, we decided to keep him. A large part of the reason was the statement I found on the bottom of the shipping bill: "All Sales Final."

But for all the confusion and turmoil of his first day in our home, the squirrel dog from Cisco Kennels in Arkansas turned out to be just as he was billed: a squirrel dog. Still he was very different from Luke. There was nothing warm or fuzzy about him, nothing loyal in the way of most dogs, no gratitude for being taken in or being fed. In fact he was downright aloof.

You could pet him, and sometimes he would wag his tail in a halfhearted way, but you could tell that in his view of a dog's life, there were more important issues than being liked. He had a reputation to defend, and enemies were constantly encroaching on his turf. Most of these enemies were squirrels. He had a mean streak, a dark look out of his eyes. It was as if he were a trained assassin—as if the squirrel population had committed some outrage against his ancestors, and he was determined to get even. If he lived long enough, he would have a hand in getting them all.

Because of this dark obsession, he had little time for anything but defending what was his and planning the death of his enemies. So we called him Clyde, after the outlaw Clyde Barrow of Bonnie and Clyde fame. No other name came to mind. Other than being fanatical about finding and annihilating squirrels, he seemed to have no distinguishing characteristics that would suggest a name.

Still Clyde was a bonanza to us boys because he allowed us to continue squirrel hunting with a dog. He always found squirrels. If he could get at them, he would kill them before we could shoot, but usually they had sense enough to take to the trees. This meant that we got to do the shooting, so the only challenge was getting Clyde to give up the quarry. He became so well-known in the neighborhood that people would come by the house and ask me if they could take him hunting even when they knew I couldn't go. And he was not particular about the people he hunted with. All he needed to see was the gun, and the battle was on yet again. Loyal to nothing but his dark purpose in life, he had a have-gun-will-travel mercenary streak in him. And thus it was that we expanded our hunting range again, for Clyde was a wide-ranging dog, and being bigger than Luke, he could cover more ground in less time.

Under the influence of Clyde, we left behind the small three-acre spread where we had still-hunted. We crossed the pastures and even went through and beyond the woods that Luke had introduced to us. We headed toward the Catawba River and the Appalachian Mountains. Our parents had no earthly idea how far into the woods we were going. And if they had, I am quite sure that they would have put a stop to it. And it was this driving deeper into the woods that finally made the threesome a twosome.

Roy's mother didn't like him being gone so long, so he started staying home. She was alone with two children, and she needed him there to watch his sister when she was busy. Cousin Jacob lived alone with his grandmother at that time—the uncle that taught him to bird hunt and to deer hunt had not yet moved back to Sledge—so he was free to keep going deeper and deeper into the woods with me and Clyde.

Every time we hunted, Clyde seemed to go farther and farther. We would mill around waiting for him to bark, and then all of a sudden, we would hear what we at first thought was an echo. We'd brace ourselves and listen, and sure enough there he was, just barely inside the range of our hearing. Off we'd go, running at breakneck speed to get to the tree before the squirrel got away.

A bark is a signal, as complex as a Morse code system. The best dogs have different intonations for different situations. With Clyde, tempo and tone were a vital part of the system. A fast tempo meant that he was certain. The squirrel was in the tree, no doubt about it. The longer the time between barks—the slower the tempo—the more doubtful he was. Either the squirrel had fled to parts unknown or maybe Clyde just smelled him and the trail was a bit on the cold side. But when the tone began to vary, when the pitch began to go up, that meant to run like hell because something was happening. The squirrel was running or so close that he wasn't going to stay there long. Jacob and I never talked about the system; we just intuitively understood it and acted accordingly. When we heard Clyde bark, we came running. When he barked fast, we ran like hell. When the tone began to vary, we ran like double hell.

So there came a day toward the end of that squirrel season, a gray day in January when it was far too cold to be out hunting, a day when I heard something different in Clyde's bark—something hysterical in the tone, in the tempo. But I never said anything about it. In fact I probably never fully formed the thought that I was hearing a different bark. It was one of those observations that comes clear only after the fact—when you look back on a day when something unexpected and disturbing happened.

What I did know on a conscious level was that the bark was a long way off, so when we started running, we soon passed through the woods on the other side of the fields and found ourselves heading into the enormous trees that came before the river. I have no distinct memory of when we knew we were in new country. I just remember the trees—huge oak and elm trees, towering over a deepening hollow that went on and on and on—and right in the center of it a thick swath of undergrowth. And I knew that we were getting close to the Catawba River, and we were no longer on Chapman land or land that belonged to anybody that I knew. The stream at the bottom of the hollow probably led into the river if you followed it far enough.

These were the only deep, wilderness woods I had ever been in, and despite my frenzy to get to the barking dog, I noticed the eerie calm they imparted. It was as if we had entered a realm where human beings were no longer terribly important. We were just another species, and our deaths would mean nothing more than the death of anything else. There were no funerals out here—only dissolving and vanishing into the earth beneath the giant trees just like everything else God created.

We followed the hollow on and on until I began to run short of breath, and Jacob, running just ahead of me, slowed to a trot and then stopped. He was breathing heavy, and he thrust his gun barrel ahead of him and down toward the ground, saying breathlessly, "Look a' that."

The hollow was evening out a bit, and the ground was plowed up here and there as if a cultivator had been through.

"Hogs," he said, "Gotta be wild hogs. My uncle down to the hunting club says they plow up the earth just like a damn tractor. I bet they all in this deep part a' the woods, headin' to the river. Damn hogs!"

The only contact I had had with wild hogs was Fred Gipson's *Old Yeller.*

The ending, the part where Travis puts the gun through the chinks in the shed and shoots the rabid Old Yeller dead, made everyone cry. But though it was sad, I got through that passage the first time without shedding a tear, and in every subsequent reading, I didn't even pause. No, it was the wild hogs that got me. And it wasn't the sentimental part that got me there—the fact that Old Yeller risks his life to save Travis from the hogs—it was the hogs themselves.

There was something supernatural about them. The tusks on a wild boar make him look like something from the jungle. And then when you add to that the fact that these creatures were once quietly sleeping in mud on somebody's farm, waiting on somebody to throw slop in there for them to eat, so they could open their tiny little eyes and ravenously gulp down what any self-respecting dog would turn his nose up at—well a feral hog was something that seemed about as far from reality as anything I could imagine.

The images from *Old Yeller* were jumbled in my brain because I was out of breath and excited. I tried to remember. Did the hogs just attack out of the blue like rabid dogs?

I didn't have long to think because Clyde's barking was moving around and getting more and more frantic. I could tell we were getting close, but I could also tell that whatever he was trailing was moving around. Then suddenly I knew that the bark was different, and I knew why.

"Jesus," I said out loud without knowing I was going to say it. Jacob, one step ahead of me said, "Yeah." Then he began to run again and I followed him—on toward the barking.

Now I would like to say that we ran on because we wanted to find the dog and protect him in wild-hog country, but though I cannot speak for Jacob, I can say that such a thought was not in my mind. I ran because Jacob ran and because the dog kept barking. I ran on some intoxicating combination of fear, excitement, and adrenaline, something that in later life I would know is an essential part of hunting: the chase. You go out there to see what you'll find. And sometimes what you find is something you've never seen, something you've never imagined you would ever see, some dark secret of the world. And in some ways, that's why you're there. Maybe that's the only reason you're there.

So while something in my brain was telling me to turn around and run the other way, I went in the direction of the bark, knowing I could not and would not turn back and run the other way. I had never run so hard in my short life, so hard that I didn't even stop to reckon where the next breath was coming from or where my feet would take me or when I would stop or where I would be or what I would be facing when I stopped.

The hollow spread out again, and now there was no undergrowth, just the giant, ancient trees, and at the bottom you could see a slow-moving creek, full from early winter rains. The hollow turned a bit to the east, and just as we completed the twist, I saw Clyde.

The barking was moving around because the dog was moving—in and out, chasing and being chased by a feral hog. Dark-colored and muscular, the boar had short stubby tusks and a thick ridge of red hair down its broad back and, just when the dog got close, it would lunge forward, with its head lowered. But Clyde was small and agile—at least in comparison to the hog—and he would dodge away and leave the hog running after nothing. The hog would turn around, then charge in Clyde's direction. And the dog would lunge at him again.

I said that Clyde had attitude in hunting squirrels, that he wanted to have a hand in killing them all. I now realized that Clyde had attitude period and wanted to kill anything that got in his way. Though the hog was four or five times his size and mad to boot, Clyde just kept charging in—tormenting, taunting, tempting fate.

Jacob was still ahead of me, and I watched as he stopped and began loading up his .16 gauge. By the time I got to him, he was thirty feet from the hog and was drawing his bead.

"No," I shouted. "You got six-shot in that gun. You're not gon' do nothing but make that hog madder'n hell and then he's gon' come after us."

He looked back at me, a puzzled look on his face, but he did lower the gun.

Then he raised the gun again, but then he lowered it, looked over my way, and nodded as if to say "you're right."

Now my statement was not based on knowledge—I had never seen such a creature before. My statement was based on pure instinct. It seemed to me that the hog was mad enough without us entering the picture. But that still left us with the problem of the dog, and he was not slowing down. When he would lunge at the hog, he would get down low, as if he were going to nip at the hog's feet. The hog would then head after him like some disgruntled rhino, and Clyde would dip and weave away like a boxer in the ring, leaving the hog out in the middle of nowhere.

Then I remembered how smart pigs are. It was a part of that pop-culture knowledge that every young man of my generation carried around. I had seen a Mutual of Omaha television special on the intelligence of animals, and this one put forward the notion that the pig ranks number one in intelligence. This was very hard for me to believe because hogs looked dumber than damn dirt, but I assumed that all I saw on television was true. So, I reasoned, if the hog is smarter than the dog, one way or the other, he's going to figure a way out of this dilemma.

"So if we don't shoot, what'd we do?" Jacob said. "Can ya call him off?"

Clyde had a dark purpose in life, and when he was hunting, he was cold as dead fish to anything but the hunted. He took us only because we had guns that could bring the animal in question down to his level. So I figured calling him off would be useless. But since there was nothing else to do, I decided to try it.

"Clyde!" I screamed, stamping my foot. "You come on here." The dog seemed not even to hear. The second time I yelled, the pig swung his head in our direction.

"One of 'em is gon' tire out," Jacob said. "Guess we just gotta wait."

We didn't have to wait long. The hog began to trot away, walking like he was ready to drop the whole matter, to let the thing die. Then Clyde ran after him again, nipping at him.

But this time when the pig turned back, Clyde's dodge was a bit off, and the hog knocked him around a bit. The pig lunged again and came very close to impaling Clyde on one of his tusks.

I calculated that this contest had been going on for quite a while now, that we were seeing only the last few moments of it. Clyde might very well be on the verge of collapsing. And it was then that I had a moment of pure logic.

Though the dog was outdoing the hog by virtue of being small and agile, he was using a great deal more energy than the hog, who was merely lumbering around. It was inevitable that what we had just seen was the first step in the demise of our dog. He would not give up—it wasn't in him—so he would tire out and the pig would kill him.

And then I performed a feat of daring and stupidity. I would like to say that it grew out of courage. I would like to say that my love for my dog was such that I was willing to take a risk for him. But neither of these things is true. Clyde was not the kind of dog you would die for because you knew that he would not return the favor. There were too many squirrels still running around in the world that he had to kill. But with the cold, hard logic of a hunter, I had realized that if I did not act, we would lose Clyde and that losing Clyde the year after we lost Luke would be too much and no damn bastard of a pig was going to do that to me.

I was running before I knew it, dropping the gun in the leaves and going straight for the pig. I heard Jacob yell something behind me. I covered the thirty yards in amazing time, and when I got there, the pig and the dog were facing one another down in one of those moments of sheer staring that are a part of every fight.

When Clyde heard my footfalls behind him, he ran straight in snarling.

I caught him just when he got within striking distance of the hog, yanking both of his back feet out from under him and quite literally pulling him out from under the charging hog and throwing him over my shoulder like a sack of meal. How the hog missed me—or I missed him—I don't know because I was too busy grabbing and turning and running.

And I kept running with the dog looking back over my shoulder and growling and yipping and snarling and shaking his head while trying to claw his way out of my arms and over my shoulder as if he would tear into that hog if he could just get free of me. But he never did. And I just ran on til I felt safe.

Then finally, panting and still trying to contain the snarling dog, I looked behind me. Jacob was carrying both my gun and his, shaking his head and saying, "You one crazy son of a bitch."

Clyde was still trying to climb over my shoulder and get down, as if he wanted to make it clear to all—God, hogs, the squirrel population—that I had stopped the fight and that he was in it for death if such was required.

But suddenly all was quiet, the fight was over, and now we had the problem of getting home in the gray winter evening.

Shadows were lengthening beneath the enormous oak and hickory trees. We had run to the barking dog at breakneck speed without considering how late it was or how we would get back. We had noticed no landmarks. I was afraid to put the dog down just yet because I had a notion he would head back to find the hog, so our progress back through the woods was slow.

We trudged on in the gray twilight, and time seemed to stretch out. Suddenly we were not entirely sure whether we were leaving the woods or going deeper into them. All trees looked the same, and the hollow with the creek at its bottom seemed to twist on forever. After what seemed an hour, we realized that we did not know where we were and that continuing to walk in what was soon going to be complete darkness made no sense at all.

We had brought no emergency provisions—no compass, no food, no water, not even a match. We had set out with only the excitement of the hunt to sustain us. Nothing else. It was a mistake I would never make again, a kind of carelessness I would never allow myself to indulge in. The lesson of the deep woods was suddenly very clear. You could die out here. You could dissolve into the earth, and no one would know where to find you.

And now the temperature was dropping, and the darkness seemed to fall in some sort of final way, suggesting that all that we did not know about these woods waited to engulf us.

We did the only thing we could. I put Clyde down, leaving him to determine his own fate. Then we loaded our guns for protection and dug down into the leaves for warmth. We would have to wait the night out.

Ever the survivor, Clyde cocked his head a bit, sniffed the ground, sniffed the air, shook himself real hard, looked us over one more time, and curled up in the leaves to sleep. I looked at him, balled up there with his tail curled around his legs and over his nose, already asleep, and I realized that he was prepared for life in the woods in a way we would never be. He too had brought nothing, but he was of the woods. We were not.

All that endless night I shivered, cursing my stupidity and cursing the damn dog, hearing the innumerable mysterious swishes and creaks and calls of night in the woods. At some point I must have slept, for the sounds faded away. But at no point did I forget how cold I was. All night, it seemed, my teeth chattered and my hands trembled and my feet were blocks of ice. And then I saw the gray of the dawn in the sky behind the skeletal tree branches. At first it was just a suggestion of light, a mere lessening of the dark, and then the sky was there, a gray backdrop for the trees.

Jacob stood up. "We have to go," he said. "My grandmother'll be frantic."

Clyde uncurled and stretched a bit. And we were off, trying to find our way home.

At noon we converged with the small search team that had set out to find us earlier that morning. Everybody was overjoyed to see us. But after an hour or two of relief, the joy subsided, and the punishments were doled out. Both Jacob and I were exiled from the sport of hunting for the rest of the season—maybe forever my mother said. And I was restricted to the house until further notice. My father threatened once again to get rid of "that goddamn Arkansas outlaw mutt Clyde." But he never did.

No, Clyde came out on top once again. The other boys in the neighborhood could still hunt, so they would take him hunting while I stayed home lying on the couch and watching one of our three television channels. Sometimes I would watch Clyde leave the yard, and he seemed to strut in a high-hipped kind of way as if he knew he had come out on top. Like he was the king of creation. He cared not one whit that I couldn't go. In fact he cared not one whit if I lived or died, so long as he was fed and could hunt.

And slowly as winter became spring, the irony began to settle in. Unlike Old Yeller, who was willing to give his life for Travis, I risked mine for Clyde and got not one damn thing for it, except maybe exile. But later I realized that this was not exactly the case. The dog would be around for next season. And I guess he'd let me go hunting with him. But there was more to it than even that. I had seen the deep woods, and something of them stuck in my mind. I knew I would go back after my exile was over. With or without Clyde, I would go back and walk among those ancient trees. But the next time, I would go prepared for the unexpected. I would reckon the cost of what I was doing.

Yes, for a second time in as many years, I had run into the woods, run headlong, spurred on by sheer adrenaline and the glory of the hunt. The first time I had thrown up and shot without reckoning where I was shooting. The second time I had run at breakneck speed, deeper and deeper into the woods without any thought of where I was going or how I was going to sustain myself if I should not be able to find my way home. In both cases I had discovered how deep and dark and mysterious the woods are. And how unforgiving. I had been lucky. Though I had paid a heavy price in losing my dog Luke, I had survived being lost and sleeping in the elements on a frigid night.

Still, even the best luck runs out. No, I would not make such mistakes again, I told myself. I would reckon the cost of what I did. The world I had seen out there was big and mysterious and scary. Yet in some strange way it called to me. I would do better when I got the chance to walk again into the deep woods. I would be ready to answer that call.

End of a Season

1962

The two ducks flew in on a breezy February afternoon. They landed in an oak tree, upsetting the order around the boy in the same way that a beautiful woman might have upset all in his world.

He was plump, pimply, and he saw very few beautiful women in his small-town world. But there was one who sometimes rode the school bus. She was a teacher and a single mother. She wore her hair in a French twist, and though she was well into middle age, she retained something of those sensual curves that the boy could have never named or even fully described but which drew him like a magnet. She had a kind of strange sophistication that he could also not have described. He dreamed of her asking him to get off the bus and follow her into the house.

He had heard of duck hunting all his life, but he knew no duck hunters. In his small town, there were only deer hunters and squirrel hunters. His father was neither. He had left the family many years before for another woman. He came back only once a year to visit; he was some sort of businessman in Denver. The boy was not exactly sure what his father did, but the boy thought it involved money. The boy's friends Jacob and Johnny had taught him about hunting, taught him what their fathers or uncles had taught them. And though those fathers or uncles hunted now and again, they were too busy working at this or that to take Jacob and Johnny hunting more than once or twice a year. So the three boys squirrel hunted in the hollow, waiting quietly beneath the huge oak trees until they heard movement and then drawing their bead.

The hollow was close enough to the houses in town so that the boys had their parents' permission to hunt there so long as they didn't go any deeper into the woods. Those woods were the great mystery that surrounded them. On the west side of town, they seemed to go on forever. There was the Chapman farm, then the lake and swamp that bordered it, and deeper still the wild woods where deer and wild hogs and turkey roamed freely. Somewhere in that same vicinity was the Catawba River. But the boy was not sure where. He was also not sure where the woods ended. He assumed that they did, but he knew that they went on into the mountains, and after the mountains, his sense of geography was jumbled.

Until quite recently, the boys he hunted with were restricted to the edge of the woods. And within those edges, the boys had been still-hunting the hollow, slowly and methodically killing most of the squirrels there.

And then they started hunting with dogs, going deeper and deeper into the woods.

And that was why the boy was there alone. His mother had found out about their forays into the deep woods and had said no.

"Roy, I need you around to help with Sister while I work. I can't go traipsing into the woods to find you. And she's too young to be left alone. You can hunt in the hollow, but you can go no farther than that."

Squirrel season would end soon, and there weren't many squirrels left in that hollow anyway. But being fanatical and lonely, the boy stubbornly persisted in wringing the last few days out of the season, even if he wound up sitting there and wishing he saw squirrels instead of really seeing them. Soon all the boys in town would pack their guns away and start planning spring fishing trips in the swamp just on the edge of the Allred farm.

So the ducks shook his small, local world. It was as if they came from deep in the woods, from the parts of the woods that were forbidden to him. They presented to him the possibility of being a duck hunter, far above and beyond the boys with whom he sat beneath the trees, the boys who had left him to hunt in the deep woods. He would do what they had never dreamed of or even imagined: kill a duck.

Seeing the ducks, the boy froze. And then he jerked his gun into place, moving so abruptly that the dry leaves beneath him rustled loudly and the ducks quickly took to the air before he could shoot, flying with surprising speed. He watched them as they angled through the trees, and then he saw them against the backdrop of the gray winter sky, flying with a steady, frenetic beat of their wings. He then heard a high-pitched chatter, almost like a cackle of laughter. It trailed behind them as they flew away. Their agility, their speed caused something within him to stir.

That night in the living room of his small house while his mother read stories to his sister in the bedroom, the boy got the *World Book* encyclopedia and looked up "Duck." And there he saw on the page of color pictures, the very ducks that had flown into the oak tree. They were wood ducks. The male was the one he recognized. His color was striking—green and chestnut and buff and white with streaks of blue and black along the wings. He looked like a painting—just as he had looked in the tree. And then, reading quickly, Roy understood exactly why the ducks had been there: they nested in hollow trees in spring and then rejoined the flock after the young were brought into the world and had flown from the nest. They were building a nest, mating.

That night lying on the bottom bunk of the bunk beds he shared with his little sister, he dreamed of ducks flying over his head. He remembered pictures he had seen in *Field and Stream* of duck hunters in a blind, of decoys, of black Labs swimming toward shore with duck carcasses in their mouths. But most of all he dreamed of killing the ducks he had discovered, for now he knew their secret. They were nesting, and they would be back.

For days he haunted that particular part of the hollow with his shotgun, awaiting their return. So intently did his eyes scan the sky that he missed shooting one of the rare squirrels the boys had left in their overhunting of the hollow. He also came to recognize for the first time in his life the first hints of spring.

He came to know the springtime as a thing in itself, a secret almost in the same way that he now knew the ducks' secret. Later in his hunting life, he would know that he had stumbled on one of the primary secrets of good hunting: to know the woods. The sounds, the contours, the seasonal rhythms that stitched life together. It was like a pulsing in the bloodstream.

But he had never noticed it before. He had never watched and listened carefully enough to discover it.

It was as if the air had lost some of its edge, as if beneath the cold, which was still there, a damp current of air foretold a kind of warmth that was calling life back into the world. The winds of winter were dry and knifelike, causing the dry brown leaves to scatter. But the winds of late February carried promises. He had never known this before, but he realized it had always been there every year of his life: this slow renewing of life step by step, the buds growing bigger and bigger each day until they exploded into leaves or flowers. He had not known to watch for it, had just assumed that spring happened one day in the same way that one day it got hot or cold, or one day it rained.

Though March was still a week away, the old gnarled oak trees knew spring was coming. Every day he saw the tiny buds protruding from the branches like small beads of sweat. And the birds were everywhere, calling insistently from tree to tree. He knew that the ducks felt it too. That was why they had come flying in. It was to answer the springtime, to respond to the change in the air. For this reason he wondered about killing them.

"Why do you keep taking your gun down into the woods?" his mother asked him on the third day of his vigil in behalf of the ducks. His mother was sitting in her easy chair, mending a pair of pants that belonged to him. She had the Spartanburg newspaper folded in half on arm of the chair. Before she had started on the mending, she had done what she did every night—read the paper from cover to cover to find out what was going on in the world. Sometimes if she found something that she thought would be of interest to the children, she would read aloud.

At fourteen the boy was instinctively secretive around his mother even when there was no reason to be so.

"Cause I want to kill a few more squirrels."

"Ain't the season about over?" His mother looked back down at her mending. Then before the boy could answer, "I thought you boys had killed every squirrel ever born within a hundred miles of that hollow."

The boy's mother had always wondered where the outdoor impulse came from in her son since his father was not a hunter even when he lived with the family. In fact he had been no outdoorsman at all. With his wing-tip shoes and his creased black pants and starched shirts and his job in banking, he could not understand why anyone would waste valuable time stalking animals to put on the table when there were good grocery stores in every town.

"Next Saturday, I think," the boy said. Actually, he knew it was next Saturday. Then after a pause, "They's a few left. I think maybe."

Just to be sure, the boy got out the yellow "State of South Carolina Game Laws" paper he had gotten at the hardware store. It was folded many times from when he checked it almost daily in the weeks before squirrel season started. He stored it safely in his sock drawer.

Right he was. Squirrel season ended on the last Saturday in February. And duck season did too.

At first this fact was of no more importance to him than noticing that the television stations now went off the air at 12:30 A.M. as opposed to 12:00 A.M. Since no one had ever offered to take him duck hunting, he had never really looked at the dates of duck season—had never really considered the question of when duck hunting was legal or not. But since he now knew that the season was still in, he realized that he would be doing nothing wrong in pursuing the nesting ducks.

He thought again of being the first among his friends to kill something other than a squirrel. He imagined holding, possessing the many-colored drake, showing it to his friends, telling them that he stalked and killed this—he alone.

He even thought of the woman on the school bus. What would she think if she knew that he, as young as he was, had killed a duck with help from no one? He imagined bringing the bird home and having his mother prepare a roast duck. The whole family would sit there around the table, and the main dish would be something that he had killed and brought home for the family. She might even tell his father. He didn't know the difference in movie and television images of roast duckling and the reality of eating a wood duck killed near a local pond, a duck that had barely enough dark meat on it for a single serving or two—little more than a good mouthful for every member of his small family.

But then he became uneasy. What if there were eggs in the nest? What if they had already hatched? What if he were responsible for killing the mother duck and orphaning the young? He reasoned that this was silly. If there were eggs, the ducks would always be there. But much like the discovery of spring among the old, gnarled oak trees, this was a feeling totally new to him. He had never really given much thought to the idea that wild animals raised their young presumably in much the same way that people did. He had never considered the orphaned young of the squirrels he had killed.

He had been uneasy many times in his life, but it had always been for a clear reason: he was doing what he should not. This uneasiness was new because he was breaking no rule. What he was doing was legal. People had to eat. Why should he feel uneasy?

Still, for several days he stayed away from the hollow. It was as if he were conquering some part of himself. He would reason it out. There were no squirrels to be had in the hollow, and if he sat and resolutely waited on the ducks, which he knew he would do, he would be faced with the decision of whether to kill them or not, assuming they showed up. It was better just to stay away.

But the thought of the ducks was like a missing tooth that the tongue looks for again and again even though the tongue knows every inch of the cavity where the tooth was. He would sit at the dining-room table and do homework only to find himself imagining bringing those ducks home. And he could not for the life of him understand his reluctance. Why shouldn't he kill the ducks? The season was still in—he had verified that. He knew where they were—he knew that they would come back. The ducks were like a gift from God.

Other times he would walk the neighborhood trying to find his friends. He thought if he found friends to spend time with, he would forget about the ducks. And then the season would be gone, and he knew that he would not even think of breaking the rules and hunting out of season. His parents had taught him to follow all rules—in town, in school, in church.

But for some odd reason, all his friends were occupied. Jacob and Johnny were likely hunting in the deep woods with Clyde, that gun-colored dog Johnny's mother had bought for him. Ronald had started taking music lessons. His mother was also forcing him to practice an hour a day. Harold was on restriction for making low grades. That left only Michael. And Michael was one of those friends you sought out only when the world had become as empty as an abandoned, weed-choked drive-in theater. Like as not, you would wind up in his room rifling through his collection of sports memorabilia and listening to him tell you about each item in excruciating detail.

Walking the streets though, the boy felt the spring moving forward with a strange insistence, as if the world were being overcome by something. The sunshine seemed more certain, the winds insistent, downright balmy sometimes. People were talking about how early spring had come this year. And then the flowers on the japonica bushes burst forth with a red color that was outrageous among the somber browns and grays of the faded winter landscape. When he saw the japonica, he thought of the bright, vibrant color of the male duck, the green and coral and orange of the drake's head. So stunning it was against the drab brown landscape, against the drab color of the female.

The afternoon was gray with high, wispy winter clouds against a slate sky. The cold had come back for a day or two as it often will in early spring. He put on his hunting jacket against the cold, put some number-four shells in his coat pockets, breeched the .410, and put it in the crook of his arm. Then he walked out among the trees that he knew so well.

Everything was quiet. He was used to the squirrels not being there, for he and his friends had killed most all of them. But the birds that had been so insistent only a week before seemed to have been chased away by the cold, gray sky. The woods were lonely in the way that winter is lonely. It was hard to believe that the world could change so quickly, so completely. From all appearances winter had won, and spring would not be coming back. It had been chased away.

He took his seat beneath an enormous hickory tree within easy gun range of the oak tree where he had seen the ducks.

He soon discovered that it was hard to wait. In later life he would realize that this was probably the most important lesson of hunting: that the waiting is in some strange way the perfection of the process. If game were always there, always immediately available, you would always kill it. Again and again and again. It would be like the buffalo out West, something he had learned about in school. Killing them was so easy that it became a pathetic, meaningless indulgence, a kind of gluttony that carried with it the seed of its own destruction as well as that of the world.

He waited for an hour. And then he waited some more. He could tell that dusk was coming despite the fact that the sun was invisible in the gray sky. And just as he was on the verge of standing up to walk home, the ducks flew in as suddenly and remarkably as on the first day he had seen them.

This time he was ready for them. He moved quickly and silently, getting his gun in place, consciously fighting against his excitement. The male perched on the huge branch that was just above the hole in the bole of the tree where the female had quickly disappeared. The drake looked around at the woods, perhaps gauging the danger. The hammer was cocked back, the gun ready to go. The boy put the bead right below the neck at the place where the white neck stripe and the chestnut-colored breast came together. He was certain that with that shot he could bring the drake down.

Later he would say something told him not to shoot. In actuality that was his description of events after the fact. Memory reconstructed the moment, tidied it up with words. In the heat of those seconds, there was no voice telling him anything. It was more of an instinct from deep within, like that of the spring itself, that kept his finger still on the trigger. It was too easy somehow, and the bird was too beautiful, too trusting of the woods, of the tree, of the early springtime. The boy quietly lowered the gun, lowered the hammer, and then stared at the bird for what must have been a long time. Then he walked away from the woods to pack his gun away for yet another season.

Years later when the boy grew up, he taught his own sons to hunt—squirrel and duck both with some success. When he would bring them to visit their grandmother, he would tell them that he was indeed among the generation of boys who hunted out the squirrel population in the hollow near their grandmother's house. But the story meant little to his boys, for by then that hollow was gone, and houses were built there. And had he told them of the ducks and his vigil in the spring, that would have meant even less, for Allred swamp and the lake where the wood ducks had lived was no more. Developers had drained it in hopes of building houses there. But the land was so low that the water came back and the project had to be abandoned. It was barren now and weeded over so that in spring, the only change was the greening of the weeds.

The Longing

1965

Jacob White, Jr.

S he was one of those women who become beautiful after you see them a few times. I was young enough not to have a working knowledge of women, but old enough to think about them all the time. So though I had never really pursued women with much success, I had done plenty of looking and imagining. So when she showed up at church, I sized her up.

It is one of those terrible habits that we men have. You rank the women your age as either hopelessly beyond your reach, within your reach, or someone you are just not interested in "in that way" as people often say. But the truth is, women never stay where you put them. Inherently smarter than we men are, they're always making your neat categories collapse like the walls of a poorly built house in a tornado.

So it was with Angela. I saw her at church, put her in category three; saw her in the grocery store, decided I might have pigeonholed her too soon. Then I saw her at church again and wondered if she hadn't exchanged bodies with a movie star. She had that subtle beauty that one comes to know in the same way one might come to enjoy the taste of a fine wine: slowly.

So I did something very uncharacteristic of me. I went up and talked to her. How we got around to hunting I am not sure. I think maybe I was trying to convince her of my manliness. And in small-town South Carolina, there was no better way to make such an argument than to bring up hunting exploits.

So she says in this offhand way, "Ever been coon hunting?"

I was too surprised to lie. "No," I blurted out. So in no less than fifteen minutes we had a date of sorts. I was to go coon hunting with her and her father and some of his friends.

I lived with my grandmother on a farm because both my parents died when I was three. I had learned to hunt mostly with my friends Roy and Johnny and occasionally my wild Uncle Ted. But I had only heard about coon hunters. Only seen them from afar. I thought of them as a breed apart from any hunters I knew or ever imagined wanting to be.

Perhaps it was because they hunted in the night. Perhaps it was the dogs—those dangle-eared hounds that sometimes cost a thousand dollars or more. If you look at him closely, a coon hound has the look of a dog that lives under somebody's front porch and sleeps sprawled in inch-thick dirt all day—the kind of dog that cocks a sleepy eye when a car drives up to the porch, only to drift quietly back into the land of nod before the car door opens.

And the hunters. They always appeared to me to have crawled out from under a rock somewhere, to have wandered into town from way out in the country, so far out they rarely get in, so far that they could hardly talk in a way that you could understand them. To this day the banjo twang of their voices rings in my ears.

Now my rather overprotective grandmother might not have been too happy about me going off coon hunting with people she didn't really know had Angela's father not been a physician. He was the pediatrician over near Yellow Bluff, and though he was not my doctor, everybody knew him and pretty much liked him.

But he did have his strange side. He was a coon hunter of course, not something that most physicians claim to be. He was also the lead singer in a country band of some sort, so that outside the office everybody knew him as "Whippoorwill" or more properly "the Whippoorwill." He even had the name on his ornate mailbox at the end of the long, winding drive that led to his palatial farmhouse on twenty acres of pristine land that had never been plowed or cut, so he claimed. "Whippoorwill" was written in jaunty letters with musical notes all around it so that the mailbox was more of a sign advertising who lived there rather than a box for letters.

I had never laid eyes on the man. I just knew all of this from town legends and stories and mostly from my uncle, who later came to live with my grandmother and me and taught me to bird hunt. But when the Whippoorwill and his lovely daughter showed up to pick me up on an early spring Friday afternoon in a huge, throbbing pickup, I added another piece of information to the mix. "The Whippoorwill" didn't look at all like a physician. He looked like the lead singer in a country band. Long, tall, and gaunt, he was a cross between Richard Petty and Hank Williams, Sr.

"Miz White," he said to my grandmother, "We'll have your boy back here 'fore dawn if we don't get lost."

I was already looking at the dogs. They were in metal cages in the back of the pickup, looking out at me with rolling, excited eyes, their noses pressed against the bars of the cage so they could get a whiff of me. I heard the low murmur of a good-natured growl or two. Then one of them whined. They knew where we were going.

"That one's mine," Angela explained.

Then she giggled in a way that made me want to reach out and touch her flesh. "Peanuckle, you hush!"

When we got to the hollow just off Highway 53, I discovered that the dogs had nothing on the rest of the hunting troop. The Whippoorwill had six stalwart hunting buddies. One of them was nearly seventy, and the others were an array of backwoods types, most of them dressed in bib overalls underneath camo jackets. The range of weights was staggering. The Whippoorwill himself couldn't have weighed more than 150 pounds in soaking wet clothes after a big meal. Some of his buddies were even thinner than he was. And then one of the men, a perpetually smiling character called "Frog" in overalls the breadth of a parachute, could have tipped the scales at 300 pounds at least.

From the cages in the bed of every pickup, the dogs whined and cavorted like circus animals waiting to be fed. But the men paid them no mind. They stood as silent as monks or cajoled one another with well-worn phrases that made me know they had been doing this a while.

"This here's Angel's friend Jake," the Whippoorwill said quickly. "He ain't never been coon hunting."

"Angela'll show him what to do," the Frog said smiling broadly. Then to me, "Just follow the dogs, that's all. It's all about the dogs."

An hour later the dogs had been released, and we all sat around a fire.

I had been in the woods at night before because I had been a Boy Scout, and I had gotten lost out there chasing Johnny's squirrel dog Clyde, but I know that I had never been completely aware of their enchantment and mystery until this night. Part of the feeling came from the fact that Angela sat beside me with a camouflage jacket and cap on and jeans stuffed in her hunting boots. I probably didn't have the language to call her sexy, but that is clearly what she was. There are certain women who gain sexuality rather than lose it when they are dressed in clothes that you would normally associate with a man, and she was clearly one of these. Her face was far too beautiful for a hunting hat, but for some reason I could not and cannot explain, the hat made her even more beautiful than she was.

The boys as they called themselves—"We boys," they'd say—talked in low murmurs and passed around a flask or two. In the light of the roaring fire, I had the sense of things unseen in the air. Men and women had sat around fires like this ever since the world began, dealing with the basic element of finding food, staying warm, staying connected to one another. They had learned to feel at one with enormous trees and the sounds of animals and the magic and danger of the night air. They had learned to see in the darkness, to hunt in packs with dogs as their companions, which is just what we were doing. Somehow I had lived in a television version of the world, and I had never known these things before. I felt more alive than I had ever been before.

It was a clear night in early spring, and the air was just vaguely damp, so that the dew would be settling in soon. The moon was one or two days from full, hanging about thirty degrees above the horizon as clear as if it were just over the hill there. Its light suffused all around us with an amber glow. Otherwise we would have been closed in by the glow of the fire, creating a ring of light in the darkness.

The dogs were all around us. Sometimes I would hear them running, and then I would hear the mournful sound of their whining and baying. Except for once in a while, the men seemed not to notice. Once or twice one of them would look over at the Whippoorwill, who sat/leaned/slumped against a huge fallen oak, bracing himself on an elbow.

"Whattcha think, Peanut?" one of the men would say.

The Whippoorwill would shake his head and say a word or two: "cold trail" or "not yet" or "maybe—just wait and see."

All the while Angela was leaning into where I was, translating for me. I pretended not to hear her at times, so she would lean closer, so our skin would actually touch, sending a thrill through my body. And after a while I caught onto a few facts.

First, the Whippoorwill's other name was "Peanut." To this day I don't know why. But I can say that among coon hunters, a man or woman might have four or five names, all used at various points in a sentence. I am quite sure that there is a grammar here that I do not understand, but I have given up trying, for I was not allowed to become a part of the brother and sisterhood of coon hunting. I was a visitor.

Second, understanding the baying, whining, cavorting of the dogs is even more complex than understanding the mystery of names and grammar among coon hunters. Good coon hunters can understand exactly what the dog will sound like when there is a coon and when there might be a coon and when there was a coon, and he has gone, and when there is no coon—all those things.

I do know that, when the dogs' baying acquired a plaintiff, almost desperate moan, the men stood up, all of one accord, and gathered their guns and lights and headed out. Angela was one of the first ones up. She motioned me to get up and come on.

Through the woods we ran—like hell! I felt very fortunate to be following rather than leading because we were bounding over rocks, through thickets, up and down hills. The Frog was not with us, I noticed, but everyone else, including the seventy-year-old man, called Hefflin, was keeping up.

The baying of the dogs was louder and then louder and even louder and then we were there. It was a sight I will always remember.

The dogs surrounded the bottom of a huge, live-oak tree, boiling around its base in varying degrees of agitation. Angela's dog, the bluetick named Peanuckle, stood on his hind legs and clung to the tree while trying to climb it. He raised his snout into the air and moaned like a man in love. But the other dogs wanted his place, so they would go between his hind legs and the base of the tree, sending him sprawling. Sometimes the dogs would fight for position, snarling away at each other with surprising fury. But the fights never lasted long, for they were transfixed by what was in the tree.

The Whippoorwill shone his light up the bole of the tree, pushing dogs this way and that, kicking them if need be, and then, when he finally saw what they had treed, he dropped back and said, "Shit!"

From the darkness around the tree, I heard a chorus of "What?" or "What'd you see?" or "I hope that don't mean what I think it means."

The Whippoorwill continued to look up the tree as if he were trying to figure out a real hard math problem.

"It's a damn bobcat," he finally said, still looking up the tree.

I felt the hair on the back of my neck stand up. I had never seen a bobcat, but I knew they were sort of like a South Carolina version of a leopard. But the men didn't seem frightened at all. Rather, they were disappointed.

"I knew it," the old man Hefflin said in a rusty, despondent voice. "Could tell it by the bark ah the dogs." It was the first comment he had made all evening.

There ensued a conversation on what to do. One of the men said that they should shoot the cat, but the Whippoorwill said no. Apparently the Whippoorwill was a real conservationist, and he believed in shooting only what you would eat and nobody ate bobcat. It was too tough and stringy.

So I realized suddenly that this meant Angela and the Whippoorwill ate coon. This was mildly disquieting to me because, though my grandmother had always cooked the squirrels and rabbits and the one turkey I had killed, I had never heard of eating coon. But the conversation continued as I thought through what was being said.

It seems that the central problem was Peanuckle. Getting him off the tree was not possible unless the animal in the tree fled or died.

The Whippoorwill was adamant on this point. "That dog," he said, "is a damn fanatic. He will not leave where he's treed unless you pull him away and then soon's you let him go, whist," the Whippoorwill gestured with his hands the motion of something whizzing by you like a jet plane, "he's back on the tree like a boomerang."

I looked at the dogs. If anything, they were more agitated than they had been when we got there, and Peanuckle was at the center of the group still trying to climb the damn tree. When he got tired, he would just lean there with his long snout pointed up the tree and his paws clinging to the bark and howl/moan with a plaintiveness that seemed almost human. He would have the cat no matter what.

By now the Frog had made it to the tree. He was breathing hard from his slow traipse through the woods carrying along his large bulk and his flashlight. He stood there gasping for a minute, head down and one arm extended as he leaned on a tree. Then he weighed in on the conversation, declaring that the Whippoorwill was right.

"Ain't no pulling Peanuckle off a tree. Naw," he said between gulps of air.

Then the cat began to move, which sent the dogs into renewed paroxysms of grief and longing. By now every light we had was trained on the tree, and you could see the cat up there. He had been sprawled out astraddle a limb panting from the chase, but now he started moving in toward the center of the tree, edging down a bit. He moved slowly and carefully like a tightrope walker, and he would pause once in a while to look down at the dogs and hiss. But move though he might, the cat had nowhere to go. There was no neighboring tree he could jump to, and if he jumped down, the dogs would be there waiting. And of course if we pulled Peanuckle away, he would head straight back the moment we let him go. The only thing we could do was give up on the hunt. And then we'd have to drag Peanuckle, kicking and screaming, back to the trucks.

And then the miracle occurred. In her quiet, womanly way, Angela proposed a solution. I was amazed that the men listened to her. I was amazed that her father let her do what she proposed. But more than that, I was amazed at her courage. She proposed that she would stand on her father's shoulders and climb onto a limb beneath the cat's perch and poke him with a pitch pole.

The chief argument for this course of action was her size. She was small and agile and could easily be lifted up. Furthermore, when she got in the tree, the men could distract the cat while she climbed. Her small size would keep her from shaking the tree. Then when she surprised the cat with a poke, he would leave for parts unknown, and Peanuckle would chase him and then give up and go on to find a coon.

The Whippoorwill again looked as if he were doing math. "Angel," he finally said, "I don't like my baby girl up in a tree wid a, a, a damn bobcat." He shook his head.

Hefflin readied the bolt action on his rifle with a metallic click. "Peanut," he said (meaning the Whippoorwill of course), "I'll have my gun trained on that damn cat and if he moves on toward Angel, I'll pop his ass." He paused meaningfully. "Be a dead cat." He looked away as if the matter were resolved.

These were action men and an action woman, so as soon as the Whippoorwill consented with a nod of his head, Angela was up in the tree with the pitch pole, and the men were making all kind of threatening sounds to distract the cat. Then just as they had planned, Angela poked the cat. She poked him hard. And he came out that tree clawing the air like somebody had set him on fire.

To this day I have never seen such chaos embodied in living creatures. The cat hit the ground already running and the dogs sprawled and lunged after him in an agony of desire and longing. I got knocked down by something—a dog, I think. And then before you could snap your fingers, the action was proceeding through the moonlit woods with the diminishing fury of a tornado moving on out of your neighborhood and taking everything with it.

Angela, down from the tree now, helped me up.

But alas the solution to the problem was not as foolproof as we had hoped. The dogs chased the cat for an hour before they could be brought back to coons, and even then Peanuckle was nowhere to be found. And without Peanuckle, the other dogs couldn't seem to find anything but cold trails.

Peanuckle showed up two days later with a rip in his chest that the Whippoorwill stitched up. But the Whippoorwill said later that Peanuckle was never the same again. "That old bobcat just took the smartass right out of him," the Whippoorwill lamented.

And I guess of the whole evening, I remember Peanuckle the most. For on that moonlit evening, I was smitten with Angela. Seeing her climb that tree in a camo jacket and a camo hat and tight jeans stuffed in her boots was the final moment when all my defenses failed. It made me know that did I live to be a thousand, I would never understand or fathom that woman. How can a beautiful woman also be a coon hunter who probably eats coon and at the same time be willing to climb a tree after a bobcat? And how can she look like that in camo? I had no answer for that. I could not even put it in words.

And like Peanuckle, longing and moaning after that cat, I was fated to long and moan after Angela. Just after the hunt, I did not know how to ask her out on a date, and by the time I mastered those challenging words, she was going steady with a football player named Greg about twice my size.

I would lie awake at night out on the farm, with my grandmother snoring loudly down the hall, longing for them to break up. I would imagine terrible tragedies befalling Greg the football player. But then when they did break up, I discovered that there were many boys my age who had likewise been awaiting the breakup. Pickup after pickup had already passed the Whippoorwill's ornate mailbox to visit Angela on that pristine twenty acres of uncut timber before I ramped up the courage to call her.

And she was with boys my age the same way she was with coon dogs and coon hunters—calm and deliberate, fickle even. She would choose somebody and toy with him for a while. But I could tell by looking at the two of them in town or at school, that she was more or less doing the same thing with him that she did with that old bobcat. Just poking at him with a stick to see what he would do. And it just made me long for her more.

And then when my turn finally came, we dated a while, but she always had other interest. Other trees to climb, you might say. I guess she was category one, out of my league, even though it took me one hell of a long time to find out. She eventually followed her father's lead and went into premed at the University of South Carolina. And I won a coveted scholarship to Davidson.

I wince every time I call home, sure somehow that my grandmother or my uncle will tell me about her engagement or her wedding. Until then she's still out there somewhere, and I'm still howling and moaning like poor Peanuckle at the bottom of that oak tree, for Angela quietly took the smartass right out of me when she climbed that tree after the cat, and I knew even then that I would never be the same again.

My Uncle's Dogs

1974

Jacob White, Jr.

My uncle died suddenly, one of those heart attacks that come in mid-stride, blockage in the vein doctors call the widow maker, only he had no wife to become his widow. She had left him many years before.

He fell right where he was—two feet out the back door heading out to feed his dogs—the old orange-ticked English setter bitch named Sam (short for Samantha) and the Brittany puppy Harlan. When my grandmother found him, the dogs were sitting on each side of him as silent as monks. Even after she called the ambulance and the EMTs got there and began working to start my uncle's heart, she said the dogs stayed there, unwilling to leave him.

And then later that night when it was all over, she called from the hospital to tell Ardie Johnson, her neighbor, that Isaac had passed. She asked him to check on the dogs because she knew Uncle Isaac would want that. Ardie later said that they were still waiting right there where she had told him the body had been. But one of them—he wasn't sure which—had been howling. He'd heard that before she called, and he'd wonder about it.

My grandmother had always been independent and capable of surviving anything: poverty, a world war, the death of her oldest son and his wife in a car wreck after that same oldest son had survived Omaha Beach. And soon after that, the death of her husband, who had been bad to drink for years before he died. And of course she had had to raise me (the son of that same oldest son who died) after she had long since raised her own children. And now Uncle Isaac, her second born, had dropped dead, and she'd found him out there in the dark all by herself. But she would have none of me staying there to help her. She was way too independent for that. There were relatives just up the road, she said. Lots of them.

But then four months later, when she told me that she was moving into town and selling the farm, something gave way inside me.

You grow up on a farm. Your body adjusts to its rhythms and somehow selling the place is like selling your flesh. This was the farm I'd known all my life. This was the farm where the father I never knew grew up. This was the farm that my great-grandfather—one-half to three-quarter Cherokee— had chiseled out of the earth with nothing but will and determination. The farm my uncle had brought back to life all those years later with me watching and helping. And it was the farm where we all learned to hunt in the same way we learned to work.

I had left at eighteen, determined to make my mark in the world. I did four years at Davidson on a full scholarship. And then I did my law degree at Boston College, graduating with distinction. I enmeshed myself in city life, becoming a junior partner in one of the near-prestigious Boston firms in near-record time. I got a nice apartment near Beacon Hill and filled it with nice furniture.

And then something happened. It wasn't that I couldn't do the work. It wasn't even that my drive and energy left as they do in people who are burned out. I just stopped wanting to do it anymore. It was as plain and simple as that. I'd had my fill of plea bargains and depositions and trials and discovery—the whole damn mess. It was as if an instinct as old as time told me to look forward to the next phase of my life. Only there was no next phase. I'd lost the map.

"Don't sell it," I exploded to Grandmother over the phone. "Not til I come home and—" I was without the right word suddenly. "And see it. Again. And stay a while."

A long pause on the other end of the phone.

"Junior," Grandmother said in her most precise way, "What about your work?" And then before I could answer the question, she added, "You know that Uncle Isaac had a hard time making a go a this place and that he came here with some money in the bank he could rely on when times was tough. He made some money off'n it, but it was a hard go. And he always had money to back him up. He was real careful."

She was a woman who never let you answer a question or finish a sentence. She thought one step ahead of everyone she talked to, especially if the person was a man. She also tended to speak rapidly, throwing all she wanted to say out and letting you sort through the details and put them in order—almost in the same way that someone might throw all the clothes in the basket on the bed and let someone else do the folding and sorting. Perhaps that was why my uncle liked the silence of the dogs so much. There was his wife who left him and took his kids. The great silence of a broken heart. And then there was his mother who talked him to death.

"My work has gotten boring. It—"

"And what about Lorry?"

"We are no more."

This time she was silent, but I could name my grandmother's thoughts. They would be something like this: *This is the fifth girl in three years.* It was actually the seventh. It amazed me that a woman in her eighties could still be a damn matchmaker. But she was.

So before she could say anything, I said, "There'll be a woman who lasts. One of these days, there will be. The truth is I just like women too much to settle on one or the other of them just yet."

"I'm only twenty-eight," I added, hoping to reassure her, but she was two steps ahead of me.

"You know that your uncle had cut back on the farming. He still had the cows, but he had pretty much stopped raising soybeans. And of course he grew that Egyptian wheat to keep the quail population healthy and the dogs happy. So he could hunt and all. You know it's hard these days to keep a family farm going. Soybeans ain't what they used to be."

A pause long enough for me to try to think of something else to say.

"You know how much he loved to hunt. I don't know what'll happen to Harlan and Sam. His dogs."

And then with no transition whatsoever: "You know that that Angela moved back to town. The Whippoorwill's daughter. You know the doctor you hunted with. Yep. She's a biology teacher over to the high school. Decided she didn't want to go to med school after all. You used to be sweet on her—you remember."

It was this last statement that she really wanted me to hear. That's why she held it until the end.

I knew that seeing the place for the first time after Grandmother left would be hard. What I didn't count on was that seeing the dogs would be harder. Nothing had been closer to my uncle's soul than hunting dogs.

Wherever he was, there was a hunting dog, trailing along behind him or lying beside him or watching to see where he was going or what he was up to. The young Brittany, Harlan, was new to me. I'd never seen him work, but I had seen him cavort around the place like a wild stallion, making me wonder if Uncle Isaac had it in him to train one more bird dog.

But the setter, Sam, was so much a reminder of Uncle Isaac it hurt to look into her brown eyes.

Grandmother'd had Ardie Johnson come in to feed them for the four days between her departure and my arrival, and I guess they expected to be fed when they heard my truck. So when I came walking around the house, they were both standing just down from the house near the barn, where Isaac used to feed them.

They both knew I was the wrong guy, and Harlan was definitely spooked. He dropped back, circling while watching every move I made. He whimpered, keeping one eye on me and another on Sam.

Sam knew me. She had to, for she'd been a part of the family for at least six or more years. I had even gone hunting with her once or twice. But she was wary too. She wagged her tail slowly, growling a little bit in a good-natured way, and then finally raising her nose and letting go of a sound that was somewhere between a bark and a howl, the dog equivalent of "I don't know about this." Harlan dropped back even more and began barking himself. He understood her language.

I gave up and fed them, figuring that if nothing else, I could win their trust that way. But they kept their distance. Eating could wait.

After I had gone in, they ate a little bit, but not much. Before I went to bed, I looked out the kitchen window. In the light from the window, I saw them lying on the back gallery ten feet apart. Harlan was sprawled out on his side sound asleep, but Sam was still wary and tense. She was lying down with her chin on her paws, but in the light from the window I saw the glint of her open eyes. She was staring off into the dark.

I hadn't planned to take them hunting. Even though I was not sure that I would stay beyond the three-month leave of absence I had taken from my job, I still had this intense need to put the place in order. Besides, I had never really been much of a bird hunter. I had been pretty passionate about hunting when I was in junior high school. I had hunted squirrels with the neighborhood boys. I even hunted coon with the Whippoorwill and his daughter, Angela—she who had now returned to teach biology at the local high school. But I never got the hang of bird hunting.

At the time it just didn't seem exciting enough. I was used to the dog treeing and barking as if he would die if you didn't get to the tree and do something. It seemed so quiet with the dog suddenly standing still as a statue until you flushed the birds. Oh I had hunted birds with my uncle, and I'd sometimes help him with the dogs, but I think he knew this was his sport, not mine.

That I had never quite taken to bird hunting was one of the many sad ironies of my uncle's life. He thought of me as a son, and in many respects he was a father to me when I really needed one. He'd come home to the farm when I was in my teens, and after a year or so of getting adjusted, we really clicked. I guess we had both lost something we couldn't get back.

As much as my grandmother tried, I always knew I was an orphan, always had this solitary sense that, when the world started falling apart around me, I had only myself to rely on. It made me strong, but it also made me lonely. And I think my uncle had the same sense of the world.

It was not that he had come up alone as I had—it was more that he had lost everything since then, and nothing would make the world quite right again. He had lost my dad—his older brother—just after the war. And then his father had died—after several years of fading away into alcoholism. And then his wife had left him for another man, taking his two daughters with her. He did his best to stay involved in their lives, going to see them every two weeks and bringing them to the farm every summer. But the everydayness without them got to him. And all that doesn't even count the fact that he had been dumped, abandoned. That has to hurt.

It was like he worked all day to keep from thinking about how alone he was. And then on the weekends, he hunted or worked with the dogs with that same furious energy. But what do you do in the evenings after supper? That's when the thoughts you don't want to think worm through and make you feel empty and afraid like the world's going to swallow you.

I would see him out there on that back gallery, staring off into the sun as it sank into the Appalachian Mountains. He would have a cup coffee beside his chair, but he wouldn't drink much of it. And if you looked at him, you knew he was a million miles away, fighting demons he didn't even have names for. And then finally about dark, he would grab the still-full, now-cold cup and say, "I guess I'll go on up to bed."

Well, in some ways it was similar with those two dogs of his when I came back to the farm. Their eyes followed me everywhere I went, not really imploring, not really accusing, just watching like they knew there was something missing. So one day I just said, "All right. Let up on me. Tomorrow, yes tomorrow, we'll go bird hunting."

The next afternoon, I found Uncle Isaac's old over-under .20 and his bird jacket. He'd been a tall man, just a bit taller than I am, so the jacket hung a little long in the shoulder and the sleeves came down midway across my hand. I rolled the sleeves up, put the gun in the crook of my elbow, and called the dogs.

I knew the gun would get their attention. Harlan was in the truck bed almost before I lowered the gate. He slid and tumbled into in a heap in the upper corner of the bed. But Sam was hesitant. She wagged her tail halfheartedly and stood behind the truck. But when I called "kennel," she just looked at me.

"Kennel," I said in a loud voice, even though we both knew she heard me the first time. She sat down on her haunches and whined a bit. And then she put her nose in the air and gave me that howl/bark again: "I don't know about this."

I leaned my gun against the truck and swooped all sixty pounds of her up and placed her beside Harlan. "Get in there, you bitch!"

I slammed the gate shut, got in the truck, and we headed out to hunt.

It was one of those resplendent October days when the trees are just beginning to reach full color and the sunlight has that soft, amber color it gets in autumn. The air was cool, but not quite as cold as it should be for October. It would have been a perfect day for hunting if Uncle Isaac had been here. But without him, it just made me sad.

Seeing the old fields that Uncle Isaac and I used to work made me wince, but this was what I bargained for. I wanted to see it all again, to be there for what perhaps would be the last time. I had taken a leave of absence to do that. Well, I had to look at it even if it hurt. It would have helped if the place had been run down or overgrown, if Uncle Isaac had allowed the fields he stopped cultivating to go back to woods. But Uncle Isaac was an engineer from Clemson—he was way, way too neat for that. The place was as pristine as it had been when I left home at eighteen.

I drove on down dirt roads beside fallow fields until I reached a wooded area just beyond the last cow pasture. I stopped the truck, got my gun, and let down the tailgate of the pickup. Harlan was gone in a flash, hitting the woods as if nothing else could really matter. I watched him run breakneck into the tall brown grass between the trees, holding his head up. I imagined his nostrils flaring, taking in the scents with that wonder you see in a young dog.

Sam held back with me, her dark eyes looking after Harlan, her nose twitching a bit.

"Quarter," I said, hoping that she would contain Harlan before he flushed every damn covey in the county. She trotted into the woods, disappearing into the grass just after Harlan.

People always say that teaching a dog to point is arresting an instinct. The dog wants to stalk the birds, and you teach her to stop in midstalk, to wait until you can come in and prepare to shoot them. Well that may be true, but Uncle Isaac always doubted it. He used to tell me that the dog understands a whole lot more than we think.

"The dog," he used to say, "has never been asked about the matter. The miracle is that the dog lets the hunter go at all. The best dogs teach you to hunt. You just have to let 'em do it."

Sam collected the wild-ass Harlan simply by walking into the woods, and when she finally pointed, he fell in behind her. She locked down real hard with her tail erect, and as I began to creep in, I kept an eye on Harlan to see if he would honor her point.

Just as I was thinking he knew the routine, Sam seemed to relax a bit, an infinitesimal lessening of the tension in her legs, and Harlan ran right through the covey scattering them to hell and back before my gun even reached my shoulder.

"Harlan," I yelled, "bad dog." I felt like throwing a rock at him, but I was too old and educated for that. Besides he was my uncle's last dog, and just as a quail dog honors a point, so I would honor Uncle Isaacs's dogs even if they did bust the covey.

And then I was struck by the embarrassing truth. I had forgotten to utter the most important word in the bird hunter's vocabulary: "whoa." They were waiting on me to say the magic word, to hold them on point with it, but I had forgotten.

The quail were surprisingly plentiful, up and down the far side of the pasture and even over the rise at the edge of the lake property where I had spent many an afternoon fishing. So the problem was not finding quail, it was working with the dogs.

I should have just put the gun down and watched them work because they really had their own system going. But I was fool enough to think that they needed me. So I kept following them.

Sam worked methodically, quartering the open woods, keeping her nose high, then getting down low and sniffing the ground. Harlan seemed to calm down when he kept her in his vision, staying beside her or behind her, watching every move she made. She pointed again in the old hollow where I had built a fort as a child. As I headed in, watching Harlan carefully and preparing to say "whoa," I saw the ruins of the fort, pine boards I had pulled off an old barn. The whole structure was lying there in disarray. I got too close to the covey because I watched the fort and not the dogs. The birds exploded in every direction, and Harlan ran after them with an enormous burst of pent-up energy. Sam just walked in where the birds had been, smelling the ground with that philosophical look that all old setters seem to have.

She pointed six times, and from all those opportunities I got two shots, missing both times.

I finally sat down and called the dogs to me. Harlan looked at me sideways, the whites of his eyes showing, his tongue hanging out of his gaping mouth like a red rubber sock. He paused for a moment, sat on his haunches, panted deeply, licked his lips several time, and then trotted off, looking for more birds. Sam came over. She let me rub her head while she panted. Her brown eyes looked over beyond me, and it was then that I realized what an imposter I was and how the dogs must have known it from the first. In my uncle's coat with my uncle's gun, trying to hunt in the same way that he had hunted: what arrogance. As if you can become a bird hunter just by picking up a gun and following the dogs. I looked at Sam's brown eyes again. What was she thinking? Was she missing him in the same way I was?

I didn't have answers to any of those questions, but as I drove the truck back over the roads with the dogs in the back, I remembered my uncle's words: "The best dogs teach you to hunt—you just have to let them do it."

It took many tries, but now as December settles in, I believe the dogs and I might make it after all. They will sit with me on the deck in the warmth of the midday sun. And when we hunt, they seem to tolerate my mistakes.

There is a rhythm to bird hunting that I never knew before. I wish I had understood it before my uncle died. But I take comfort in the fact that I have begun to understand it now. Perhaps it's his legacy to me. It has to do with understanding the dogs, sensing the rhythm of what they're doing and letting yourself go with it. Perhaps the birds are even onto it—I don't know. It's like so many other rhythms that I have discovered on this place since I've come back home.

Sometimes after we have hunted, I will call the dogs to the truck, and we will sit and watch the late autumn sun set across the pasture. The dogs seem to know that it is now time to rest, and they will go to sleep as I let the farm come back to me like someone I used to know. I can't understand its language just yet, but maybe someday I will. I just know that it is talking to me some place deep inside, creating meanings where meanings need to be, giving me back something that I lost long ago. I feel very close to my uncle at these moments. And now I know why he came back. He lost a lot in his life, but he didn't lose the woods. The dogs made sure of that. They reminded him of what was left after it seemed that everything was taken away.

I resigned my position in Boston this week. My savings will run out in six months, and I will have to figure out what to do with the rest of my life. Right now I think I'll stay here, for I have discovered that something of this place is in my blood. But my grandmother is probably right. I can't really expect to make a living on the farm. Besides if I have learned anything, it is that my uncle knew more than I do, even though like most engineers, he could not find the words to tell me. He just tried to show me—how to hunt, how to get through hard times and loneliness some kind a way. In some strange sense, he was like the silent rain that comes in the night. You never hear it. You just know it's been there and brought things back to life. And perhaps in that way he *was* my father, perhaps in that way he spoke for the father I never knew.

Yesterday I saw a law job advertised in the local paper: county attorney. I am sure it pays nothing like the job I had in Boston. But I would get to stay here and let the world happen around me. Since I don't have a map anymore, I'll just have to see what develops.

I have also started seeing Angela, my old coon-hunting friend. It has gladdened my grandmother beyond description. But I have learned not to try to predict the future or to answer too many of my grandmother's questions about my intentions with her. I guess we will just see what develops.

Uncle Ivory

1993

Johnny Chapman

I was never exactly sure how Uncle Ivory was related to us Chapmans, only that he was. I know he wasn't my father's brother or any close relation. But I know he was related to us some kind of way, though he was a Wilson. And that his real name was Ivor and that we called him Uncle Ivory because nobody ever heard of a real person named Ivor. It sounded like some count or something. And I know that he had the finest bird dogs anybody had ever seen and that he knew how to train them like nobody could. It was like he and the dogs knew each other's minds on some kind of level.

I also know that he had not moved back to South Carolina until after he retired from his job as a professor up in Virginia. He and a black fellow name of Eric from Chicago bought up a bunch of land—paid cash for it though most of the money came from the black fellow Eric. They were gonna raise and train setters, even make a hunting plantation or something.

My best teenage memories were of hunting with Dad and Uncle Ivory and Larrie, my older brother, and Eric—after Dad finally started letting me go along. Sometimes Elvin would go along too, but he was mostly too young those days. Those hunts—it was like walking among the gods.

Dad was the best shot I ever saw until the alcohol started to hurt his steadiness and his speed, and Larrie was just about as good. They had that famous Chapman steadiness, hand-eye coordination, whatever you call it—perhaps it was a byproduct of the muleheadedness, something else they both had a lot of.

I could never keep up with them. I was always slow on the uptake or leading too much. Slow and patient, I was, like my mother. I was much better at squirrel hunting because you had more time to set up your shot and all. And old Uncle Ivory never cared much for the shooting part. He just went along to be with the dogs and to be sure that they did all he had taught them to do.

But Eric, old Eric, he was the patient one. He would spend time working with me while the others went on ahead.

"What you doin' standing like you Davy Crockett or something. Hold your cheek against that barrel and sight down it. Yeah, yeah—that's it. Make it so you can turn and move and still keep it in line with your cheek and your eye."

He taught me how to hit a quail, something my father pretty much expected me to learn on my own. But even then I knew I'd never be as good a shot as Dad or Larrie. They just had that natural hand-eye coordination.

Now Dad is long gone, moldering in the ground for years right beside Mother and probably still arguing with her about his drinking. If anybody took anything to the grave with him, then Dad took a bottle of Jim Beam. And now Larrie and I are men, and Elvin has moved off to Alabama. And old Uncle Ivory—he must be pushing ninety. Aunt Molly, his prim and proper wife, has been dead for at least five years. And we don't go back to what's left of the farm up on the Piedmont near Spartanburg to hunt as much as we once did. Fact is, it's been years.

So I called old Uncle Ivory up and told him that we'd be coming out to the farm to hunt this November.

"All right," he said without hesitation and just as clear as a bell. It was as if we did this every two weeks. Then, "You know I don't cook breakfast anymore."

Truth was he never had—Aunt Molly had.

"That's all right," I said. "We'll stop at Doug's."

"And you know they ain't as many quail as they used to be. I do my best, but they just ain't there like they used to be. Too many farmers have sold out to developers. And there's the fire ants."

"That's all right," I said. "We just want to get out there and hunt again."

Doug's was in Sledge, near where Larrie still lives and where we both grew up. And it's about ten miles from the farm, and even at 5:00 A.M. on a Friday morning out in the middle of damn nowhere and in the middle of a good old-fashioned South Carolina cold snap, it was bustling with hunters—most of them deer hunters in camo. And the waitresses were vaguely attractive in a sort of honky-tonk way. They were wearing tight jeans and sashaying from table to table, pouring coffee, and talking about local politics and movie stars and how hard it was to get up in the morning. And Larrie was trying to hide his hands between his legs so I wouldn't see that they were shaking.

You see, old Larrie didn't just inherit Dad's skill with a gun. He had also taken up with the bottle, and so his wife, Ellen, had called my wife, Marla, and told her that he was finally on the wagon and asked if I could make the days pass a little faster. So—the call to Uncle Ivory and the return to the farm. This is Larrie's second wife. He drank and caroused through his first marriage. But now on his second time around, he's got two little boys, so we're all interested in seeing that he settles down.

When Aunt Molly was alive, Uncle Ivory's farmhouse was like something out of *House Beautiful*—not a speck of dust anywhere and everything neat and put away. She wouldn't have thought of letting one of Uncle Ivory's beloved English setters into the house, and he constantly complained that she'd throw away his hunting magazines and his newspaper before he half read them because she couldn't stand the clutter.

"Can't have nothin'—not a damn thing with that woman around," he would tell Dad.

And Dad would say something like: "Fore it's all over they'll have us all disposed of and cleaned up after. Won't even be a memory left to clutter up the house." He was referring, of course, to all women but especially to my mother and her harping on his drinking—even hiding the Jim Beam bottle.

Well when Aunt Molly died, Uncle Ivory took back the house, and at nearly ninety he was going strong, like a wind that just wouldn't die.

I walked in the door behind Larrie, and the setters came from everywhere. One nosed his way out of a closet, and another jumped down from Uncle Ivory's leather recliner sitting right in front of the television in the wood-paneled den. I was looking for Alice, the orange-ticked setter, the one that Uncle Ivory always talked about on the phone, the one that was descended from dogs we had hunted with as children—this was like Alice the third, fourth, fifth, or something. There had always been a setter named Alice in Uncle Ivory's life.

She was right where I thought she'd be—under the table curled up at Uncle Ivory's feet. And he sat there like the king of the world, eating a bowl of steaming instant oatmeal with way too much brown sugar and butter on top and four pieces of bacon cooked crisp in the microwave the way he liked it. He was wearing huge, baby-blue flannel pajamas with green penguins on them and fur-lined bedroom shoes that looked like somebody had skinned a possum and turned the skin inside out. I am sure that Aunt Molly would not have allowed the pajamas or the slippers, and I can't much blame her on that one.

Alice thumped her tail against the floor, sniffed the air, but stayed put.

There was a roaring fire in the fireplace in the wood-paneled den, and that old house was warm as toast, so warm that I knew it was going to be hard to leave. We had a cup or two with Uncle Ivory, talking about bird dogs and how damn cold it was and how Washington was coming undone just like always and the country going to hell in a damn handbasket. I let my eyes walk around the room. I never much liked Aunt Molly's neat version of the house. Still I had to say that Uncle Ivory had turned the place into a junk heap.

There were hunting magazines and newspapers and books stacked everywhere. Uncle Ivory read constantly when he wasn't training his dogs or watching his one or two favorite television programs. The table where he sat to eat had only one open spot—that place where he sat with his oatmeal. The rest of it was stacks, stacks, stacks. No wonder he couldn't have us to breakfast. There was not a vacant spot at the table for us to eat.

But it was nice having the dogs in the house, and like hunting dogs everywhere, they adjusted to whatever was there. They ambled around from person to person, sniffing us up and down, and looking toward the front door down the hall. We had left our guns in the truck, but they knew something was up, and they were waiting to see what it was. One sight of the guns and they'd be uncontainable.

"There oughta be quail in those thickets down by the old cattle pasture. But you gotta go in easy and give the dogs plenty of time. There're not as many as used to be," Uncle Ivory said, shaking his head.

He sipped on his coffee and didn't say anything for a minute, looking at the dogs.

"Damn, it's hard to keep quail around these days with everybody clear cuttin' and building this and that and destroying the ground cover."

He took another sip of coffee. "Hawks are hard as hell on us out here, and Eric's not here anymore. He sold his part of the operation."

He shook his head and looked at Alice. She had gotten up and stood by the table slowly wagging her tail, looking toward the front door and then back at us.

"Old Eric. I miss him something fierce. But he finally concluded that a black man in South Carolina was not viewed in the same way as a black man in Chicago, particularly when it comes to quail hunting and field-dog trials—something that doesn't happen much in Chicago. The old timers around here think that the black man is there to drive the wagon and handle the dogs. They can't believe that he owns the place. So I suppose our idea of having a hunting plantation was ahead of its time. And since he left and Molly died, I just don't have the energy"—he paused and drank deep on the coffee—"or the money to keep pursuing all that."

Well, old Uncle Ivory could outtalk anybody except Aunt Molly, so I sort of edged him on toward the idea of the hunting in a gentle kind of way. We had all heard about Eric's decision and then his departure many times, and though we missed seeing him, we didn't need the details again.

"Yeah," I said grabbing his shoulder, "Well, we not gon' give you up just yet. We still want to see them dogs a yours work. And I miss old Eric as much as you do. He's the one taught me to shoot quail."

"Yeah, yeah," he says almost as if he had forgotten about the dogs. "Well, they know not to rush in, but with me or Elton or Slick not there, they might show out a bit and try to bust the birds—if they find any. You gotta calm 'em down. Steady 'em."

Elton was Uncle Ivory's farm overseer, and he helped him with the dogs when Uncle Ivory needed it. He was Eric's cousin. And Slick, a friend of anybody who hunted quail, was out there as much as he could be what with working and seeing after his family and getting a bit old himself. But Uncle Ivory did most of the training—always had and always would, he said. Til he died. And then the dogs and the farm were to go to Elton and Slick. That was in his will.

How does a near ninety-year-old man train bird dogs, I was thinking. But somehow he had. We crated Jake and Jerry, the two young dogs, in the back of the truck. We had a third crate in the truck, but when we called "kennel," Alice headed for the cab as if there were some things she just didn't do.

And so with Alice sitting on her haunches in the cab between us, looking out the windshield to see where we were going, we were off, bouncing over the ruts in the fields, the ruts of the rows from thirty or forty or fifty years back when the man who owned the land before Uncle Ivory had grown cotton.

By now the sun was a thin line along the eastern horizon, and you could even see the faintest hint of the Smokies like a thin, gray shadow along the horizon to the west. If you just glanced at the horizon, you might think it was a huge cloud of some sort.

We parked the truck, got the dogs out, and headed toward the thickets down heading to the river, just like Uncle Ivory had said. There were no more cattle in the pasture on this part of the farm, and here and there were patches of icy snow left from an early November howler. But the cold came in and got you, reminding me that it would soon be too brutal to be out here.

Still we had dressed right and the walking warmed us up, and pretty soon, I was remembering how much I loved to hunt. One of the best parts of this life is an old double-barrel shotgun that you've had forever. I still had the .20 gauge I had saved up to buy when I was sixteen, and it seemed to fit my hands the way an old hat fits your head so that it's not even there.

We said nothing much other than things like "it's shitfire cold," but it was good being with my brother.

The first quail caught everybody by surprise, even the dogs. It was a single, angling out of the edge of a thicket, causing the dogs to turn and freeze all at once.

Boom! Boom! We both shot, but the bird was gone, not even a feather falling.

Larrie looked after the bird, and I could tell what he was thinking. That he should have brought him down. Just like Dad, I thought. He didn't say a lot, but he had to win every argument and bring down every bird. It was a hard life carrying around that kind of pressure.

The dogs were already over it though, and they were beginning to quarter. Alice was in the lead and the two young males, Jake and Jerry, were following her. Their snouts low and their tails high, they were covering ground.

"It's all right," I said. "We ain't been in a while."

"Shoulda had that one—he angled off right in front of me."

"Well, we both missed."

Uncle Ivory was right. There were quail in the thickets, but not as many as there used to be, or at least that's what my memory told me. And the trick was to stay on the edge of the woods and get them to fly into the open so you didn't have to try to hit them when they were flying among the trees.

"So how've you been, Larrie?"

"All right, I guess."

We walked on, keeping our eyes on the dogs.

"I guess Ellen told you or Marla one that I been trying to stop. She's been on me pretty good, you know. I don't think it's a problem, but she does. Says I gotta decide 'tween her and the kids and it. Damn sure seems like a man can't have no fun in this world. Can't come home from work and have a drink or two to sorta settle in."

Like Dad, Larrie's one or two was usually three or four.

"There're some that can and some that can't," I said, feeling strangely assertive for a younger brother. "Drink, I mean. You remember Dad. He shoulda stopped. He never—"

I didn't finish the sentence because Alice was frozen, her tale erect, Jake and Jerry hunkering down and backing her up.

"Whoa," I said. "Easy girl."

I decided to let Larrie have this one, and when we eased in, the dogs held and suddenly three birds flushed and rose like phantoms.

And damn if Larrie didn't miss. Perfect shot, and he missed. I knew that I could have gotten one of those.

He was mad as hell this time. "It's all right," I said. "We're both a little rusty at this."

And then I remembered how Dad's timing had faded. It's a strange thing about hunting. You have to be like the dog—attuned to everything, so that you know about when the bird is going to flush, and about how fast to bring up your gun, and how much to lead, and when to pull the trigger. And all in one smooth motion. It's really quite an intricate process, and like everything else in this life, including living itself, all of it is poised on the edge of a knife blade waiting to fall apart. A trembling hand, a sudden cloud over the sun, or even an uncertain mind can ruin it.

Untiring and single-minded, the dogs were already back at it, dragging us along no matter how many birds we missed.

I could tell Larrie hadn't liked what I said about his drinking, comparing him to Dad and all, so I shut up, and we just hunted.

An hour later the day was turning out to be overcast and the cold wasn't letting up at all, the wind blowing fierce and steady from the north. There was even a little bit of thin snow and sleet in the air. I knew we couldn't stay out here much longer. Larrie had missed two more birds. One of them was flying into the woods that fronted the river, a particularly hard shot. But the other one was part of a covey that rose and flew out low across the field. When we were kids, he would have brought that one down in a flash—probably gotten two.

To make matters worse for Larrie, I'd gotten one out of that covey. It was not a real hard shot, but it was good for me. And it was our only kill.

So when the dogs froze again, I was thinking how Larrie needed to get this one to even the day out, to make sure he didn't go home mad as hell and fall off the wagon. So as we eased in, I was behind him and far to his left, planning to let him shoot, hoping that his aim would be true.

But the small covey flushed, flying close together, and we both shot at close to the same time, probably at the same bird. So when only one bird fell, I said, "Good shot, Larrie." I'd been out of his range of vision, so I'm not even sure that he knew I fired.

He didn't say much when Jake retrieved the bird, but I could tell he felt better having at least one bird in the bag.

It's amazing how your childhood never leaves you: the same battles, the same conversations recycled again and again over and over and over all your life. I was fighting my own battle, wondering if I should lay claim to the bird after all so I could say that for once in my damn life I had skunked my older brother.

But instead I said what old Uncle Ivory used to say to Dad. "Well I guess that about does it."

And Larrie used Dad's line. "Sure as hell looks like it."

And then I remembered one of Eric's lines. "It's not about who kills what or how many. It's about feeling alive and being together."

As we headed back to the truck, the dogs kept hunting. They were all three dead tired, tongues lolling, but they still wanted to hunt. It was in their blood, and they would do it until they died. And a happy life it must be: being able to focus so completely that all else in the world is blocked out, and there is just the thrill of the chase, only that. The closest I could come to that was the way that old shotgun felt in my hands. And that could only last a few moments, a precious few moments.

Back at the house Uncle Ivory was watching *Regis and Kathy Lee,* still in his baby-blue pajamas with the green penguins on them. We had left the dogs on the porch to drink water and cool down.

"We each got one," I said before he had time to ask that question that comes at the end of every hunt—how'd you do?

But he was not interested in what we killed.

He hit the mute button.

"How'd the dogs do?" he said.

Poachers

2000

"Poacher dogs," Randy says, moving his dark glasses up onto the top of his head. "Read an article about bear poachers in the *New York Times.*"

"What's a poacher dog?"

"Bear dogs in this case. The bastards let five or ten dogs go, all with high-tech radio collars on. The collars have sensors so you can tell where the dog is and if he's barking or looking up like he would be if he treed. So these rednecks go off and drink beer or smoke pot or watch television—whatever the hell they do. And then when the control unit tells 'em that the dogs have treed, they get their guns and go after the bear. All they want's the gall bladder. Sometimes they'll take the hide and the teeth and the claws. But the gall bladder goes for five thousand dollars. It's an aphrodisiac in Asia. Big money. Bear claw soup's a delicacy in Korea."

He draws the "Ko" in Korea out, pretending to be more southern than he really is. Lummy has noticed that Randy often becomes more southern when he's involved in any endeavor that has to do with the woods.

Randy raises up his shirtfront enough to scratch the hairy roll of middle-age fat that has been developing around his middle. He lowers his dark glasses over his eyes and watches the two dogs. Randy reads the *New York Times* every day and often shares its contents with those who don't, which would include Lummy, who reads no newspaper at all.

"Do the math," he continues as the two of them watch the dogs. "If four dogs tree, then they get four bears and four gall bladders. Do that every weekend all season—that's some cash. If the poachers are unemployed bums—which they often are—they can hunt all week. If they really brazen, they hunt all year, go after 'em in the den, butcher the damn bear right where they kill him, get what they're after, and leave the carcass to rot. Move around a lot."

Two of the dogs are milling around the campsite, noses to the ground, following scent paths. One appears to have a good bit of black-and-tan hound in him, though he's too small to be purebred. He's so skinny that his rib bones show, and his neck and head are scarred and nicked.

"Some ol' bear somewhere whacked him around a bit," Randy observes, still following the dogs with his eyes.

The other dog appears to be so many-fathered that identifying his breed is well nigh impossible. Still, the dangle-eared, sad-eyed face suggests a bloodhound or two somewhere in all those fathers. He too looks a bit on the lean side as if he has not been too long escaped from a concentration camp.

The black and tan stops dead in his tracks. He noses Lummy's REI coffee filter, filled with coffee grounds and left beside the fire pit from breakfast. He crunches down on it.

"Damn you, mutt!" Lummy says.

The dog tears off into the rhododendron that grows along the creek. He hides behind the leaves, crunching grounds and filter.

Lummy runs down the dog, kicking into the bush at him. The dog emits a loud yelp and tears away as Lummy retrieves his filter. He turns it over in his hands, examining the fang marks that have punctured the screen.

Lummy Chapman is very particular about his coffee, likes to linger over it. Cannot imagine camping without fresh ground coffee. It's his payback for sleeping on the hard ground, for teaching his recalcitrant son to fish.

"Yep," Randy says in a mild, contemplative tone. "Poachers. Keep the dogs hungry and they'll be sure to keep their noses to the ground until they find whatever's there—even coffee grounds. Damn a man who'll starve a dog!"

The November camping and trout fishing trip was Lummy's idea, or to put it more accurately, his wife's. She had been on him to take his son, Wilson, trout fishing for months. But as the weekends of summer passed, filled with this and that, the trip never materialized. Then there was football season, and Lummy never liked to be gone for a University of Georgia football game. Then with Doris still at him, he finally identified a weekend when Georgia was not playing only to discover that it would be early November—after trout season ended in October.

But he decided it wouldn't matter that much. Snowbird Creek in North Carolina is an old bootlegger's area—remote enough so that they would almost certainly not encounter a game warden. They would camp there and fish—probably wouldn't catch anything anyway.

It was not the first time Lummy had cut corners. He had driven with an expired driver's license for a year or two before he finally got pulled over for speeding and had to pay a large fine. And in his youth he had acquired notoriety for shocking the fish over at the reservoir near Yellow Bluff. He almost went to jail for that one, so the story goes. People in Sledge still talk about all the bass and bream and catfish floating white bellied and stunned on the surface of the reservoir.

"Enough to feed the five thousand," one church member noted. But Lummy's father, Reverend Eddie Chapman, intervened and got the judge to reduce his sentence if the boy would do community service.

After they got into the woods, Randy had noticed that there were no delayed harvest signs on the creek and he became concerned.

"We're breaking the law by fishing here," he said with a concerned look on his face.

"It don't matter," Lummy had said. "The delayed harvest part is up that way less than a mile or two. It's the same damn fish. And we ain't talking catching that many." He pointed vaguely upstream, hoping that the part of the creek he pointed to was delayed harvest.

Randy didn't like breaking the law—he was a punctilious sort of man and an ardent conservationist. But there was little he could do. They were in the woods now, and both of their sons had hiked ahead of them to pick a campsite.

"Well, let's not tell the boys," Randy said. "I like to set a good example. Can't expect 'em to follow the rules if we don't."

And then lo and behold, they had caught fish. A good number of them. Then suddenly it was as if someone had let a truckload of mongrel dogs out. They came from everywhere, all wearing elaborate radio collars with plastic antennas.

They splashed into the creek, barked at them from the bank, trailed them and bellowed at them as they moved up stream. Most of them finally left, but these two hung on—because both boys had felt sorry for them and given them beef jerky. Now Randy and Lummy are back at the campsite, trying to figure out how to get rid of them.

Lummy shoos the dogs, even throwing rocks at them. The dogs scatter one more time. Lummy is already thinking about a morning in the cold November woods without his coffee. He picks up another rock and throws it in the general area where the dogs disappeared.

"Bastard!" he screams.

Then he and Randy head back to the stream. But the dogs show up again, trailing the boys. So by five o'clock, they give up and head back to camp with two or three illegal trout, hoping the dogs will vanish in the night so they can get in some fishing on Sunday morning before they pack up and leave.

"Surely they call 'em home at night," Lummy says.

Randy shakes his head. "You'd think, but who knows?"

Randy builds a nice fire and pours bourbons for the two of them and Coca-Colas for the boys. Lummy takes a drink of the bourbon and preps the trout for cooking. Twenty feet away, sitting on haunches amid the rhododendron, the dogs pick up the scent of the trout and start following his every movement with hungry eyes.

The November darkness falls and with it the temperature, but now both Randy and Lummy are on their second bourbon, and the fire is crackling and beginning to put out heat.

Lummy begins to feel pretty good about life. He really does like sharing the woods with his son and his friend, he tells himself. It just takes a nudge to get him going—that's all. And Doris is always up for nudging him this way and that. Perhaps in the end, it's what he needs. Otherwise he would lounge in front of the television drinking beer and watching football all fall long.

The dogs position themselves just outside the circle of light made by the fire. Every now and then, Randy and Lummy see their eyes catch the light. At just the right angle the phosphorescent glow of the dogs' eyes make them look like hungry wolves gathered at the edge of the circle of light cast by the fire, their eyes glowing red, waiting to gobble up whatever they can find—whether it be food scraps or stray campers.

Still the autumn evening casts its magic, helped along by the bourbon: warm fire, fresh trout, good stories, good friends. By the time the meal is over, both Randy and Lummy have forgotten the dogs. And it is not until they let the fire die, turn on their headlamps, and suspend their food in a tree for the night that the dogs begin milling around again. And this time both Randy and Lummy notice that the radio collars are gone.

"What happened to the collars?" Lummy stammers.

Ed, Randy's boy, speaks. "They were riveted on, so we cut 'em off with a knife. Set the dogs free. We've decided to take these dogs home. Take 'em to the vet. They're hungry. You should see the way they eat that—"

"Hell no!" Lummy interrupts in a hoarse, surprised voice. "These dogs belong to someone else. You had no damn right to cut those collars off."

Wilson, Lummy's son, pipes up. "But they're hungry. You said you should never starve an animal. I heard one of you say that."

"Yeah. Sure. Well—we've already got a dog. And we've done fed these."

No great fan of dogs, Lummy is in a tough spot, thinking about Harold, the mutt they already have, thinking about the chewed-up coffee filter, thinking about the fact that neither he nor his wife has ever figured out how to get Wilson to take care of Harold beyond smuggling him into his bed at night to sleep.

But Randy's mind has already jumped to a tougher spot. "What'd you do with the collars?" he says.

Each boy holds up a radio collar. He grabs both collars and heads off to throw them in the creek.

"Randy," Lummy calls, "What're you doing? Those things are water-proof."

Randy turns around. "I don't wanna stay here with those collars or those dogs! We gotta get outta here. We don't know who—they'll come looking for the collars and find us with their dogs. Damn those dogs!"

"Calm down," Lummy says. He's thinking of the trouble of packing everything up and hiking the two miles back to his Suburban in the dark. He's also thinking of the fact that the dogs will surely follow them and that they might even meet the bear poachers in the dark on the way to the trail head.

"The best thing to do," Lummy reasons, "is to stay the night and hope the dogs go home. We can get up early tomorrow and head home. But we need to do something about them collars."

They try to disable the collars by smashing them with rocks or cutting at them with the small knife the boys used to cut the collars off. But they can't seem to get at the electronic devices inside layers of rock-hard plastic and rubber. So after much discussion, they return to Randy's original idea: they walk up the creek as far as they dare in the dark and throw them in the water.

"I don't like polluting like that," Randy says. "But it'll take a hell of a lot longer for somebody to find 'em in the water than on land. So I guess we got no choice in the matter."

They come back to the fire, shine their lights on the dogs, and now both of them throw rocks at them. The dogs calmly watch the rocks fly by without moving a muscle. It's as if the dogs have concluded that the two are just about as bad at throwing rocks as they are at fishing. The dogs settle in again, chins on paws, their eyes glowing in the light of the head-lamps.

Randy makes sure the smoldering fire is safe for the night. Then Randy and Lummy go to their tent and the boys to theirs.

But as soon as they zip up their sleeping bags, the night comes to life for Randy. He hears footfalls coming their way, hoot owls warning of intruders, the rustling of leaves, pops that could have been distant gunshots, trees groaning in the night sounding like human voices. And then Lummy begins to snore and drowns out everything else. Randy falls into a series of restive dozes, waking up with a start every hour or so until he finally gives way to exhaustion and enters a near comalike sleep somewhere near dawn. He dreams of bear poachers with chest-length beards and ponytails of graying hair congregating around huge fires in the woods, celebrating their kills with bourbon and gin while shooting .30-30 rifles into the air.

At first light Lummy puts on coat, gloves, and hat, then peeps out of the tent. He looks to the left and to the right. No dogs. He looks to the spot on the far side of the fire, the last place he saw them. No dogs. He crawls out of the tent and stands up. No dogs. He scans the area around the tent, even looking up in the trees. No damn dogs!

Feeling as if the last half of yesterday had been a bad dream, he decides he can make coffee despite the chewed-up filter. He washes it out in the creek, using Camp Suds. Then he turns on the camp stove, puts some water on to boil, and presses the torn screen of the coffee filter together so as to cover the holes left by the dog's teeth.

The coffee is not perfect. The chewed-up filter lets grounds through into the cup. But it's still coffee even if it's a little crunchy here and there.

He's halfway through the first cup, getting ready to put some more water on to boil, when he hears people coming. Since the dogs have vanished and the cut collars have been disposed of, maybe even disabled, he knows that running away will just make him look guilty—even if these people are connected to those damn dogs. So he sits back to wait and see.

They're all three dressed in camo, and two of them have what appear to be .30-30 rifles. One of them is old, and the other two are young, but beyond that, they seem almost identical: lanky men with sharp, grasping eyes. They come straight toward the campsite.

"Seen a black and tan?" the older man says in a scratchy drawl. He doesn't exactly come into the campsite, but he moves as if he would if he should need to. "Old black-and-tan looking thing."

"Yep, there was some dogs milling around the creek yesterday when we were fishing." Lummy nods toward the fly rods leaning against the clothes rope tied between two trees. "We're fly fishing."

The older man looks at the fly rods and nods. One of the younger men leans his rifle against a tree and pulls out an elaborate electronic control from his camo coat pocket. It looks something like a divining rod until he unfolds the three antennas along each side. He begins to adjust the knobs on the handle.

"They close—somewhere right in here."

Lummy feels his chest tighten as he watches the man point in the general direction where he and Randy disposed of the collars.

The old man puts two fingers to his mouth and lets go a shriek of a whistle that could crack the sky. Lummy hears Randy stir in the tent.

Lummy is too scared to breathe. He feels his heart thudding away in his chest. He expects the two dogs to come tumbling out of the bush in all their uncollared glory, still hungry for beef jerky.

But all is quiet.

The younger man with the control unit walks up to the old man. They both examine the read-out on the device.

By now the third man has joined the group, casually looking over the antenna man's shoulder at the electronic display. He has his rifle on his shoulder on a leather shoulder strap.

"Strange," he says in a loud whisper.

"Unless somebody cut the goddamn collars off," the old man says.

By now Lummy's mouth is dry, too dry to speak, so he takes a sip of coffee and grounds and tries to look unconcerned.

The old man looks at him for a moment. Lummy holds the man's gaze, but his shoulders are trembling inside his coat.

"Yep," the old man says, "It's happened before. Some a these asshole tree huggers'll feel sorry for the dogs, think they hungry, and cut the damn collars off."

The old man continues to look at Lummy as he talks. "A dog with a full stomach. That dog won't hunt. He's gon' lie down and take a goddamn nap 'fore he does anything."

"Yep," Lummy agrees. "Sho' 'nough."

The man with the gun on his shoulder is shaking his head. He casts a glance Lummy's way. "Them things're expensive," he says with a grimace. "The collars."

Then the old man adds with a strange menacing chortle, "Somebody's gon' get hurt. That's all I gotta say. Somebody's gonna get hurt. That's all. We talkin' money."

Lummy sips coffee and grounds, sitting still and looking straight ahead, holding his coffee cup tight to keep my hands from trembling. He hears the creek flowing and sees the sun begin to shoot bars of morning light through the trees.

"Them mutts probably just laying out," the man with the control unit says in a mild, consoling voice. "They'll turn up."

He folds the antenna up and stows the unit away. Then they all three gather up their gear and head up the trail in the general direction of the cut collars.

"Give a holler if you see a dog," the old man calls to Lummy.

"Yep."

"Much obliged," one of the younger men says.

"You know trout season's done over," the old man calls over his shoulder as the three of them walk away. "Over in October."

Lummy hears Randy move around some more in the tent. With some effort, he sits still until the sound of the men walking fades into the woods. Then he looks around to be sure they're gone and finally zips opened the fly and then the tent flap. Randy is inside sitting up and looking pale. Before Lummy can say anything, he hisses, "We gotta get outta here."

He's already gathering equipment and stuffing it in his hiking pack.

"Get the boys," he says over his shoulder. "Go on. Get the boys."

When Lummy unzips the boys' tent, he sees something that makes his blood run cold. The dogs are curled up at the back of their tent. They have smug looks on their faces as if they have found more beef jerky.

"Damn you, Wilson, Ed—both you damn boys. Damn you!" he hisses trying to contain his screaming voice. "Them dogs—"

It's hard to know what to do, but Randy says they should hide the dogs in the tent as long as they can and then pack it, load up, and sprint as fast as the thirty-pound backpacks will allow.

"Out of these goddamn, Carolina bootlegger woods," he hisses.

All the way back to the Suburban, Lummy marvels at those damn dogs between wondering if he will be shot in the back and stifling the urge to scream again at the boys. *Those crafty bastards,* he thinks. *They had not responded to the crack-the-sky whistle because they knew a good thing when they found it. They were hiding out.*

The last mile is a trot, nearly a jog, because the closer they get to the car, the more convinced they become that their luck will run short and they will hear the crack of a rifle.

And now they're winding out of the mist-damp Smokies over corkscrew roads, and the two boys are in the backseat of the Suburban, each with a dog, and Randy and Lummy are arguing over who'll keep the damn dogs.

"I don't need a dog," Randy says. "I already got a dog."

"But your boy was the first to feed 'em," Lummy says. "Sides, I got a dog too."

"That's not what Ed says. About the feedin'. Anyway, you can't keep a boy from feedin' a hungry dog." Randy pauses for a moment, catching his breath before he continues.

"Furthermore the whole damn trip was your idea—you talked me into it. Talked me into staying against my better judgment. Outa season. I knew we should have left when I discovered trout season was over. I don't know why I let you talk me into it. I knew it was wrong. Knew it. Knew it. Knew it!"

And as Lummy looks over at the fog-cloaked Appalachian Mountains, he is remembering his preacher-father for some strange reason.

And then Randy pulls out his trump card. "It's just like when you shocked them damn fish. I remember that I do. No, I wasn't around then. But I've heard. So in a way I remember it."

Well now Lummy's thinking what his minister-father said to him some time back then. "If you tell one lie, Son," he said, "you gon' have to tell five more to cover it up. It's like the lies cling to you like fleas. They multiply and follow you, and eventually they cover you up."

And Lummy is thinking that his father was a wise man and that the wages of sin are sitting contentedly in the backseat ruminating on beef jerky. So he guesses he will take those damn bear-poacher dogs home with him until he can think of something better to do with them, someone to pawn them off on. Harold, stupid mutt that he is, will have friends.

"I don't know what Doris gon' say," he says, though he pretty much does know what Doris is going to say. She is no fan of dogs of any kind, any more than he is.

"We already got a dog," he says again.

"If you're gonna be a poacher," Randy says as if he's quoting scripture, "I guess you'll be needin' poacher dogs."

The Lost Antlers

2008

L arrie Chapman wanted antlers, a big rack of antlers on a noble deer head. Wanted them for his living room to make up for the ones that his former wives had one by one thrown out.

Last day of the season and cold as he had ever seen it in South Carolina, and he was the only one who had not gotten a buck that year. Both his grown sons had gotten two each, and each of the men down at the hunting lodge had gotten at least one. Still he was buckless. He sat in his tree stand and looked across the gray winter landscape. Looked at his watch. Looked back at the woods beneath him. Looked down at his Remington. Felt the cold come after him. Took another sip from his bourbon flask, then slipped it back in his pocket.

There was no shortage of deer. Fact is they seemed to be taking over the whole damn country. In the summer they ate his tomatoes when they were still green, even ate the hostas his ex-wife had planted along the front walk—down to nubs in the ground. He could hardly go out the door to his house without seeing several lumber off into the trees surrounding his subdivision. If he didn't live inside the city limits, he could have nabbed one from his deck. But when he got his deer rifle and mounted his tree stand out in the woods at the hunting club, he saw nothing at all.

The cold made his arthritic knees ache, made his shoulder ache from the wound he had gotten in Vietnam all those years back. Every few minutes the wind would get up something fierce and stir the leaves on the ground into the air; then they would fall as the wind died away. But only the wind and the leaves moved. No deer.

When his two sons, both children from his second marriage, dropped him off at the stand two hours earlier, they had wished him luck.

"Got all your stuff?" Lonnie asked. He was the younger one, redheaded just as Larrie Chapman had been when he had had hair, the one who still remembered to worry about him.

So he had checked his backpack one more time—canteen, field glasses, power bars, ammunition, cell phone, matches, flashlight.

Clayton was leaning over from the other side of the front seat of the pickup. "Three hours," he said. "We be back. You be ready." He held up three gloved fingers. There was some basketball game or something he wanted to watch early that evening. "Get your damn deer!"

They waited until he walked down the ridge and got safely in the stand before they drove off. He watched the wisp of white exhaust smoke hang in the air as their truck disappeared along the old logging road that ran along the ridge.

The last years had been hard. It started with his heart attack five years earlier. Damn near died. He remembered lying in the hospital with his chest split open—a quadruple bypass. The doctor listed the things he could no longer do.

"You gon' have to lay off the beef and the French fries. Lay off the salt. No pork. No pizza. Big Macs are out. That sort of thing. And this drinking your wife is telling me about—it has to be curtailed."

His then-wife, now ex-wife Martha was standing by the bed, arms folded across her chest. She looked like a cross between a schoolteacher and a prison warden.

"Glass of red wine a day is fine," the doctor continued, looking at Martha. "If you can hold to that. But no more of these nights out with the boys. No more poker nights. You gon' need to stay home. Rest. Exercise regularly. Walk the neighborhood with your wife."

Larrie Chapman wanted to spit in the doctor's face. He hated people telling him what to do, conspiring with his wife to limit his freedom.

Instead of spitting, he tried to be funny and also take a jab at the cold-as-ice Martha.

"How 'bout sex—that's exercise, ain't it? Can we do that?"

Silence.

"It's fine," the doctor said, no longer looking at Martha. "But you might have a little trouble in that area. Blood-flow issues. If you do, there's some medicine I can give you. But let's wait—"

"I ain't never had no damn trouble in that area," Larrie inserted. Martha looked at the floor.

The doctor didn't tell him that his balance would be shot too. That he would always be just a hair or two from dizzy, that he would sometimes fall. So that even climbing into a tree stand the way he once had was beyond his power. Now he carefully mounted each step, got up there, and spent a few minutes just letting the world settle into place. And the whole time he was up there, he felt if he moved too fast, the world would tumble about, and he would fall.

And then there was his vision. No matter what eye doctor he went to, no matter what glasses he got, he didn't see the way he used to. He had lost count of the deer he had plain missed or just not noticed until it was too late.

And now he and the wife—the third wife, that is, the one who had recounted his sins to the cardiologist, the one who had looked away when he mentioned his prowess in bed—had decided to call it quits, so he was newly single.

He told himself that he was glad to be rid of her, glad to be through with women once and for all, to reclaim his house, a house he had built mostly with his own hands when he was a young man before his dwindling income had forced him to sell most of his land and before the burgeoning city had incorporated and digested everything around the small scrap of land he had retained. Yes, he was now a part of a suburb.

But the nights with no one there—they were long and empty. Sometimes he would stare at the ceiling for two hours when he woke up at three in the morning. Remembering happier times. Remembering when his children were young and his wives were young. Remembering when he was young and strong. But these nights were better than the ones in which he regretted the mistakes he had made.

But there was one way in which the women he had married had mistreated him. They had one and all hated the mounted deer heads he had insisted on above the fireplace. And in that insistent and conniving way that the women he had married all seemed to share, they had managed to throw out his deer heads, send his antlers to the dump. When he looked back through the haze of years, he had no distinct memory of how or when this happened. He just knew that now, the place above the fireplace—it was bare. So he was here to reclaim his antlers.

There was a lull in the wind, and suddenly something moved fifty feet to his left. He got the field glasses and scanned the hillside leading down from the ridge, and there it was.

A deer in a thicket of trees and shrubs. Though he could not make out if it was a buck or a doe, he saw part of the right rear flank. The deer moved again, giving him a better view of its flank. He could tell it was large, but he still couldn't see the head.

He got into position, clicked off the safety on his Remington, and lined his scope up, waiting for the deer to move so that he could see the head. But the deer stood still.

He blinked his eyes several times and squinted, trying to see more clearly. The gray afternoon, the shadows of the tall trees, the buff winter coat of the deer blending with the brown winter leaves—all of it made the deer come in and out of focus.

After several minutes of holding still, he felt dizzy. A strong gust of wind moved the tree branches, and the leaves on the ground began to blow into the air again. Then suddenly coyotes were yelping in the woods behind him, and the deer was moving. And now he saw there were two deer. And all in a rush, the heads came into view amid a mosaic of branches. He saw antlers, and he squeezed the trigger.

The sound of the shot echoed in the cold, dry wind. The coyotes quieted and the wind died away.

He got the field glasses and scanned the area back and forth, but there was nothing there where he had shot. The wind picked up again—low, mournful, whining.

Gut shot, he thought. *Gut Shot.*

Something about the sound, the feel of the shot had made him think that. And now there was no carcass.

Down from the tree stand with his gun strapped to his shoulder, he found a spot or two of blood on the leaves where the deer had been; saw what could be tracks in the leaves heading off down the hill. He looked around him. Yes, the deer would head downhill, the very direction toward which the wind was blowing. Might fall thirty yards down the hill. Might last longer. And if he were losing blood, he would eventually seek water. There was a creek at the bottom of the ridge—he thought.

He looked at the bare trees, the descent down the ridge, the gray sky. In hopes of finding a buck, he had moved his stand to a new part of the two-thousand-acre track the hunting club leased, so the country around him was unfamiliar.

He looked back at the tree stand, so he would not lose where he was. He walked a few steps down the hill, just into the copse. Adrenaline could take a wounded deer a hundred yards, two hundred; then he might die instantly. Fall in his tracks.

Twenty yards into the copse, and he saw more blood, and now he could make out the old game trail that headed down the hill toward the creek probably a mile or so below. It was overgrown, but in the dead-winter foliage it was easy enough to follow, so he took one more sip from the flask to warm himself and moved on, keeping his eye on the ground, looking for blood and tracks.

After ten minutes following the trail, he noticed that the wind had quieted a bit and he felt warmed up. He looked back toward the tree stand. He couldn't see it, but he knew where it was.

The game trail had turned east ever so slightly, which meant that he had wound around the ridge, below the old logging road that ran along the ridge top. All he had to do to get back was follow the trail and look west.

He looked at his watch. He had eaten twenty minutes of his remaining hour. He calculated the twenty minutes it would take him to get back. That meant that he could track the deer for ten more minutes and still have time to get back before his sons would be there to pick him up. If he found the carcass and it was the big buck he had been seeking, they would help him get it back to the truck. He knew he couldn't do it by himself. He didn't have that kind of strength anymore.

But as he looked down the game trail, he could see nothing that resembled blood or hoof prints.

Then he heard something off the game trail, something moving in the brush farther down the hill. He got his gun in position, waiting.

Nothing.

But he had heard something. He knew that. So he looked back up the game trail and positioned himself so that he would know the way back to the tree stand. Then he walked down the hill to where the movement had been. And there was blood on the leaves, a circle of blood. He knelt to examine it. There was bile in the blood—the end was near. He was close.

Still, when he looked all around him, he saw nothing but woods, and here there was no trail to suggest where the deer had gone. Not even any tracks in the deep leaves.

He crept down the hill, still holding his gun in his hands so he could fire if he saw the deer moving away.

Five minutes later he looked at his watch. His sons would be at the tree stand to pick him up in ten minutes. The cloud-cloaked sun was fading in that sudden way it does in winter, casting the world into shades of gray and black. He looked at the sky and the skeletal trees outlined against it. He was cold.

So close. A bit farther down the hill. Then he would turn back. But five minutes later the darkness was such that he knew he would have trouble seeing the deer if it were more than ten feet in front of him. He took one final look around, saw nothing, and turned back up the hill.

"Goddamn," he said to the dusk. "Busted season." He sustained himself with a long draw from the flask, felt it warm him as it went down. Then he started trudging back to the tree stand.

He had not figured going uphill would be so hard. In fact, as he struggled to catch his breath, he realized that he had not figured on going uphill at all so intent he had been on finding his buck. And he had left his pack with his water and his cellphone and his matches and flashlight in the tree stand.

He set his eyes in the direction of what he took to be the tree stand and pushed on up the hill, feeling his age with every step. He had not walked thirty feet, trying to find the game trail that would lead him back to the tree stand, before he tripped over the deer carcass.

The leaves were soft and he rolled over, then stood up, grabbing for his rifle, which was still strapped to his shoulder. He saw in the gray dusk that there were no antlers on the deer he had stumbled upon. It wasn't even that big. He knelt and grasped at the deer to be sure this was the one he had hit, the one he had been trailing.

It was still warm. And there it was, the wound in the gut, still leaking blood and no antlers on the head, not even buttons where the spikes would come in. He pulled the deer's legs apart and saw that he had killed a doe.

"Shit!"

He put his gun down and dragged the deer off into some bushes, staggering with the weight of the carcass and the wind, which had picked up again.

By now the darkness was falling all around him, and he had no time to chide himself. He listened for his sons—their voices or the engine of the truck to guide him back to the tree stand. He looked around him to see if he could see headlights. He called their names over and over again as loud as he could.

"Lonnie!"

"Clayton—I'm down here!"

The wind swallowed the sound of his voice. Then it blew harder.

He fired his rifle into the air several times. But still there was only the moan and whir of the wind.

He shouldered his gun and started up the hill, pushing as hard as his patched heart would let him go. But he was gasping for breath because he was going nearly straight up, and the wind was blowing against him. Surely the path he took searching for the deer was not this steep. He didn't remember any part of the ridge side being this steep.

After ten minutes more, he stopped and scanned what little he could see of the woods. No game trail, no hillside, nothing familiar. It seemed that he was in a country he had never seen before.

He felt icy terror in his stomach, in his groin. The spittle in his mouth had a metallic taste. He remembered that taste from when he was pinned down in a rice paddy in Vietnam. He stood there trying to fight back the wave of terror while the world began to tilt and spin.

Then it was dark, dark night all around him. No moon. No stars. Clouds cloaking the sky. Still the whir of the wind as it pounded. There were matches and a flashlight in his pack, but he had no idea where the tree stand was. He might be miles from it now. How long had he been searching for this deer? It seemed to have been forever.

And when he listened for his sons, all he heard was the relentless wind—blowing, blowing, blowing against him as if it would blow away the world and everything in it.

He remembered a story he had heard of a man making it through a cold night lost in the woods by gutting the large deer he had killed and huddling inside the empty body cavity in so far as he could. But the deer he had killed was not big enough for that, and he doubted that he could find the carcass now. Besides his knife was in his pack in the tree stand.

He lowered himself to the ground and huddled against the trunk of a large tree. His mouth was dry. He grabbed for the flask. But as he tipped it up, he discovered it was empty. He cast it away.

"Shit!"

He settled down against the tree. He then heard a chattering sound and realized it was the chattering of his teeth. And there was the moan of the wind again and then finally, in his ears, the tap, tap, tap, tap of his patched heart as he shivered, huddling against the tree trunk.

Call Me Bubba

2010

Elvin Chapman

Call me Bubba. I won't tell you my real name 'cause certain people might read this and come looking for me. All the names here have been changed to protect the guilty.

I take people hunting down here on the coast of Alabama. But this year these lawyer types who are the backbone of my business—the hunters I work with every year—have become the damn bane of my existence.

My specialty is the autumn dove hunt—there's nothing quite like it. September and October are something to behold down here around Mobile. The heavy heat and humidity vanish as if someone flicked off a switch, and the air is cool and breezy without ever getting cold.

Have you ever seen the sun going down in October on the Gulf Coast in Alabama? The land is flat so that the sunset seems to last forever. The long, slow descent, the honey-colored light angling through the pine trees. Makes you think that God himself is coming to see you, walking in the cool of evening sort of like he did in Genesis.

But these lawyers I take hunting get worse every year. Times are hard down here. Now I know that everybody says how things are getting better with the economy and all, but seems to me it's a real slow improvement. What's more, folks ain't the same as they were before the crash. They've become ornery and mean. Greedy.

Take these lawyers. They're big spenders. They compete all week for clients. Or they argue against one another in court. You think they'll come out here and play nice? They're all crack shots. You get one of these boys on a spree where the birds come right to him, and he hits every one. Well, the others are pissed 'cause he's beating them to the limit. He's going home from the hunt in time to watch Alabama whip up on Georgia or South Carolina, bragging all the way.

So they go to moving around from the stands I put 'em on, seeing if they can find a better spot. While there's shooting going on, I mean.

I put them on the stands with their dogs and blinds and come back towards evening, just to be sure the farmer's land hasn't been messed up, and I can't find nobody. And then I hear 'em shooting down there amongst the cows. And I got to go get 'em, hoping I find them before the farmer does.

So I talk safety with everybody at the beginning of the hunts. Bring hot coffee for everybody so they'll all listen. I tell them that we're here to have a good time and that there's no need to be greedy about the birds. There's plenty for everybody. Safety first. Respect for the farmer's property. Respect for the law. They have to shoot above shoulder level at all times—no exceptions. Second, they got to stay where I put them. There's cows and property all around them. This is not my land and not their land. We're both paying the farmers to be here. Then I get them to sign a release.

Well this afternoon, old Marvin we'll call him, one of the big-time lawyers, leans on the hood of his black Range Rover and reads over the release and looks back up at me.

"I'll sign this, Bubba. But you know a man can't sign away his rights. In court this paper won't be worth shit." He's holding it up between his thumb and his index finger like it ain't worth shit now.

Arnie, we'll call him, his archrival, is standing right across from him, leaning back against his Tahoe, stroking the head of his yellow Lab, Bambi. He smiles and says, "Go on and sign it, Marvin. Go on and sign the man's document, Moondoggie. Ain't nobody goin' to court over a dove hunt."

Then he adds with a low chortle, "Course you might."

Everybody laughs.

"Well Arnie, I guess you should know. You the king of the frivolous lawsuit. How 'bout that case about the Ten Commandments, the one you lost all those years back? Made you the king of the frivolous lawsuit. Everybody's still laughin' about that one. Google 'frivolous' and—"

"Well, we're still appealing that one, and at least I have a sense of values, at least I've read over the Ten Commandments. Betcha can't even name three of 'em."

They can go on like this forever and everybody standing around and winking at one another, just enjoying the hell out of it 'cause it looks like they're joking.

But I know they aren't. I know that when those dove come flying in, they gonna be counting every kill the other one makes, watching each other's dogs to be sure they don't retrieve the wrong bird. Each one wants to hit the limit before the other. And let one of them miss—well, watch out. You'll never hear the end of it.

So they sign the form, and the whole time I'm thinking that I need to come back early today. I don't want 'em to think I'm checking up on 'em—they don't like that—but with them two, I need to do just that if I'm going to keep being a guide. Not get in trouble with Miles, the farmer who owns the land, or Ely, the game warden, or with God himself, who looks down over Alabama with some suspicion. It's always been a rather cantankerous state. I can say that 'cause I'm originally from South Carolina.

We load up in trucks, and one by one, I set them up around a large field where Miles grew sunflowers in the summer, spacing them out so that if they stay put, nobody's going to get hit even if they do shoot low. There's a stiff wind, so the birds'll be flying high, hard to hit. Most of what'll be coming in today will be mourning dove, but there might be a few ringnecks or white wings flying with them.

The killdeer are already beginning to sound the alarm, flying in large circles and making that plaintive, nasal KILLD-E-E-E, KILLD-E-E-E sound. I get the men all set up and I park my truck at the edge of the field and lean against it. The sun's already past three o'clock, and it's taking on that amber hue. It looks so good I wish I was out here with them. I do love to hunt, and for some damn reason I seem to have put myself in a position that I never have time to go.

My father always said that mistakes come in three parts. There's the mistake itself, the stupid thing you do, and then there're at least two consequences, sometimes more. Sometimes you make a mistake that just keeps on giving consequences, like some goddamn golden goose gone haywire, spitting bullets instead of eggs.

My mistake was taking the buyout from the rather large southern company I worked for. They moved me down here to Alabama from South Carolina some twenty years back. The company had fallen on hard times, and they offered several of us a lump-sum severance package to retire. So I thought about being able to hunt all the time during the fall and fish on the bay during the spring and summer. I was seeing the honey-colored afternoon sun on those autumn dove hunts. Feeling the brisk air. My wife would still be working, and she wouldn't be there telling me, "Bubba, do this," and "Bubba, don't do that." Kids are grown. I got to thinking that I was just invited into paradise. Why wait?

Well that money had hardly hit the market 'fore it started wastin' away. There was the mortgage crisis and the stock-market crash and all those other gyrations and spooks the market has been through over the past few years. And my wife mumbling, "I told you not to do it, Bubba. Told you, you bone-headed son of a gun."

So I had to start looking around for something to do. And that's when it hit me. Living down here on the coast just outside Mobile for the past twenty years, I know a whole lot of farmers. So I'm thinking, they got the land, and I like to hunt, have even hunted on their land—all I need now are corporate types from Mobile who'll pay me big bucks to take them hunting. I became the middleman, the guide.

Well consequence number one is that I have to deal with this group of pain-in-the-ass lawyers who are always pushing the limit. Add the oil spill to the mix (Thanks, BP!) and the slowly recovering bad economy, and it makes everybody mean and ornery. The game wardens are feeling it too.

So are the farmers. Hard times in Alabama. And I'm stuck smack dab in the middle of all three.

These game wardens in Alabama—they don't much like guides. They like hunting the old way—just a person and his gun and maybe a dog or two. Still, the first few years I did this, I didn't see a game warden anywhere. They spent the autumn at the Waffle House guzzling coffee and talking football. Not that I was breaking the law, mind you. I just didn't have to worry about 'em, that's all.

Then all of a sudden, here they come. I know what it is. State coffers are beginning to empty out. Tax revenues are down, so the game wardens need to levy fines. They're taking a close looksee at things they used to just drive by without even a glance. Well the state coffers are filling up again—but real slowlike. And the game wardens ain't goin' back to the Waffle House. I guess the state boys figured they needed to work like the rest of us.

And the farmers? With the drought and the stagnant economy, they got used to scrapping the bottom of the barrel and getting splinters under their fingernails just like everybody else. So they want those dove to be flying their way, so people'll hunt their land. One-hundred dollars a gun. They're going to improve their business much as they can.

Have you ever read the law on baiting a dove field? It's about clear as goddamn mud. You can hunt migratory birds in a field that was used for agricultural purposes so long as the leavings that the birds come for are a byproduct of the agricultural business. Now how do they make that judgment?

These farmers aren't stupid. Yeah, they planted the sunflowers. And they just happened to plant them in this one place where everybody dove hunts every fall. No, they didn't sell any sunflower seeds. They just like the way they look. Or the market wasn't good this year. Or they'll chop 'em up for the hogs. Or they didn't fill out right 'cause of the drought. So they plowed 'em up right at the beginning of dove season. Hey, it's harvest time. Yes, the grain piled up a bit here and there. Plowing is tricky. Not perfect. Well, it's enough to drive a man crazy—especially a man who wasn't ambitious or smart to start with, a man who wanted so little—just the freedom to hunt and watch the sunset.

And life is short my friend. My brother Larrie died on a deer hunt winter before last back home in South Carolina. He was bound and determined to get him a deer, and he wandered off into the woods chasing a deer, got lost, and died of a heart attack brought on by cold and stress. Died underneath a tree. His boys found him, but it was too late.

'Fore long that'll be me. Yes, sir. That 'll sure as hell be me, and I'll have spent the last years of my life worrying, what're supposed to be the best years, stuck between crazy lawyers and greedy farmers and fat-ass game wardens. And I don't even want to talk about my wife.

Well, enough bitchin' about my life. I get in my truck and drive off, making a mental note of where everybody is so when I come back I can check to be sure all is on the up and up. I run a few errands; check out a few of my other hunting spots just to see how things are stacking up for the next few hunts I'm involved with. And then long about five, I head back to check on my hunters.

Most of the vehicles are gone, which is exactly what I was hoping. It's moving on toward sunset, and people should be loading up and heading home. But two of the three remaining are the Tahoe and the Range Rover—Marvin and Arnie. Well, damn my prophetic soul!

Heading into the field I see Drew, one of the more sedate of the attorneys—he's got family money, so the economy hasn't made him as frisky as it has the others. I roll down my window and lean out.

"How'd you do?"

"Got only half my limit—took a while. Seems like they not as plentiful as they were two weeks back. And the wind." He shakes his head.

"Just you and Arnie and Marvin left?"

"Yep, but I ain't seen those two since long about four. They gave up on that field you put 'em in."

By now Drew is heading off toward his car.

I crane my head out the window. "Where are they?" I shout.

He shakes his head, looking back over his should. "Back over toward the cows."

"Shit!" I say, loud enough for Drew and God both to hear.

So I gun the truck and head down the side of the field where everybody's supposed to be. I get to the gate at the other end.

Well at least they closed the damn gate. I open it, drive through, and then close it. And damn if those rascals aren't in that field either. But I hear them shooting—pop, pop!

When I find them, they're two fields over and down a hill, and here's what I see. The cows are all bunched up over at the far edge of the field. They all give me that spooked cow stare like they don't want to be here anymore, not with two lawyers shooting shotguns in their midst. I can't say I blame 'em.

And so there Marvin and Arnie are, spaced out on either side of this little old narrow field where Miles lets his cows graze toward evening. And they're hunting on either side of this huge old tin-roofed outbuilding that Miles uses to store hay. The building is so old that the clapboards are weathered silver and gray, and some of them are warped and pulled out of the studs.

So I'm walking over toward them, trying to control my temper. "Men," I say louder than I intend, "this won't do!"

And it's then that I see Ely. It's amazing that I'm just now seeing him 'cause he's a big boy—more than a deuce, deuce and a half, I'd judge. And I see that damn game warden Ford F150 parked in front of the outbuilding—the other side from where we are. Yeah, he drove in the back way from Highway 11 on the other side of the farm—that crafty bastard. When I get up to where he's at, he's rubbing his hands along the silvered wood where someone has just sprinkled it with birdshot. The wood is bright yellow and splintered where the pellets hit.

"You got you some frisky hunters here—Miles know about this."

"I told 'em to stay in the field where I put 'em." I point back over toward the field where they were supposed to be.

"Yeah, well, they didn't."

"Men," I say, even louder this time. "This won't do, damn it!"

They both head over toward us with that yellow Lab Bambi skulking along.

"But that ain't what worries me," Ely says. "That's between you and Miles. Look a here," he says, walking around to the front of the building.

And there they are—all those sunflowers from the field piled up in front the building.

"I never gave them permission to go to this part of the farm—Miles don't know they here. And I didn't know nothing about them sunflowers."

Ely takes his cap off and examines it for a minute, running his hands along the sweatband, and then he puts it back on and adjusts it real careful-like. He looks over at the sun, which is sitting on the horizon by now. Then he looks at me and at Marvin and Arnie, who are now standing beside the building.

"Men," he says, "Looks like we got a baited field here, and I'm gonna need to see the paperwork on this hunt—them forms you had 'em sign, along with everybody's license."

"We didn't know about those sunflowers," Arnie said, and for once Marvin is nodding in agreement.

Ely's looking off again, adjusting his cap, taking it off and putting it back on. "It's your responsibility to know, boys."

Then he looks at me: "Yours too—to know where they are—even if you gotta stay out here with 'em—that is, if they signed on with you as their guide. Signed the form I mean."

Well I guess you just can't outrun bad judgment.

I look at the sun, huge and golden on the horizon, feel that cool, autumn edge to the breeze, and think how beautiful it would be to see it hanging there on the horizon if I were out hunting by myself—by myself without lawyers or game wardens or wives or farmers or oil companies or anybody else to clutter up my damn life.

"Been watchin' you, Bubba." Ely says. "Now whyn't you go on over and get me that paperwork?"

Gobble, Gobble

2011

Lauren Chapman Jones

There's a cabin back in the woods on my family's land—back there on the part that borders the sixty acres that my father sold to a real-estate developer.

The real-estate developer was going to build a huge subdivision. He got started on the other end over near the highway—as far away from the border to our land as he could get—and he built and sold about twenty houses. Upscale sorts. And he started feeling so good about what he was doing and counting the money he was going to make that he went on and cleared the rest of the land and put in the power and water and the roads for the rest of the subdivision. Just gobbled up trees and hills and everything that stood between those houses and our land.

And then boom—the housing crisis hit, and nobody wanted to buy a house. He went damn near broke for about two years, still strutting and talking all the while about how, when the market came back, he was going to do this and going to do that. Well, the market didn't come back and then he went sure nuf broke and the bank got the land, according to my daddy. So it just sits there now like some kind of forgotten dream—roads, power grids, and survey stakes overgrown with high grass and no sign of people. It's at least a buffer between the houses he did build and our land or what remains of our land.

And the turkeys love it. It's perfect—close to our woods so they can roost and nest and yet open enough for feeding and mating. And no people. The turkeys strut around like landowners. And in my way of seeing the world, they do own it 'cause they were there before that stupid-ass real-estate man gobbled it up. They were there even before Mama's people had the land.

Well, that's another story. As I was saying, there's this cabin on the land. It's built of logs and according to family stories, my mother's great-grandfather built it as a hunting lodge. Back in those days, there were no subdivisions, no real-estate men, only farms and towns, and the woods were everywhere—everybody's backyard. They were full of game, and the men would go out and hunt in order to supplement the food they got from the cows and pigs and vegetables and the chickens they raised.

You go in there and you can still see the old fireplace made out of stone. Mother used to say that they dragged those rocks up from Sledge Creek and used the creek water and sand to make the mortar. How she knew all that I don't know. Fact is I don't know if it's true or not. And I don't much care. It makes a nice story. I like to look at that old house and think about all my ancestors coming there to hunt. The land is in my blood, and I hate that my daddy sold out some of it to the subdivision man.

The house is in remarkable shape for something so old. I think the logs are something like cypress, so according to my daddy, they're not going to rot. And the roof beams are huge—they appear to be oak or something. And the roof itself is shingled in cedar shakes according to my father. But here and there you can see where people have repaired it—added chinking to the walls, replaced shingles that blew off in a storm. It's like everybody who came here participated in keeping the house up, and now they're gone and all we can do is see where they've been.

My brothers like to remind me that it was my male ancestors that came there to hunt and that the women stayed home and did the cooking.

"And so what happened to you?" they'll say—half kidding and half not kidding. "You related to Annie Oakley some kind a way?"

I tell 'em, "Just 'cause I can outshoot you don't mean I'm related to Annie Oakley. Just about any idiot can do that."

But for all that, I can't complain too much. They do let me hunt with them without too much back talk. And though Daddy was stupid enough to sell some of Mama's land, he does have a sticker on the back of his Z-71 truck that's just for me. It's pink with a buck's head and antlers outlined above the caption "Girls like to hunt too."

"That's my baby girl," he'll say, smiling at me.

Well every year since the real-estate developer lost out, we've done pretty well with turkey hunting, each one of us getting the limit most years. We use that old cabin as a reconnoitering point. Except this year I've been too busy to go, trying to finish up high school and get in a good college. I've also got a rather demanding boyfriend that I'm half-a-mind to cut loose. But the men in my family are now saying we've got us a gobbler blight on our hands. They can't seem to call nothing up, so they've decided that the gobblers and the jakes are "all henned up" because we had an early spring and not much of a winter.

Men are bad to complain—at least the men in my family. Since my mama died of breast cancer six years back, I am the only woman among three men. It's a hard life. I'm always having to set them straight about this or that. They almost never admit that they've been set straight, but you can see it in their eyes if you look real close. It's like they stop focusing on anything in particular and just look away at nothing. They know I'm right. They'll never admit it, but they do.

Turkeys are smart—no doubt about it. But the hens are smarter than the gobblers. It's my theory that if the hens were the ones that people hunted, there would be very few kills. But gobblers are men, and if you know men like I know men—living with three—you can call up a gobbler during mating season.

So I set out to do just that on a Saturday late into April. Nobody else wanted to go because they said they hadn't had any luck. Those boys don't have any patience. So I got up early, put on my gear, painted my face, and got my Beretta camo-colored automatic .12 and headed out.

We've cut blinds and hiding places all through the woods bordering that open area, but when I get out in the woods I see that nobody has cleaned them up this year. They're a bit overgrown with springtime briars and weeds, but I find one in a likely spot, set my camouflaged stool up, and wait.

If I do say so myself, I am the best turkey caller in my family, and a lot of the birds my brothers have killed have been roused and worked by me. I don't much use a box call or a slate call. I mostly use the mouth call, the diaphragm. That way I can do the call without moving anything but my mouth, and I have more control over the sound. It's like I become the hen. But before I do any of that, I try to become a part of the woods. That's the most important part. And that's what I love about turkey hunting—you aren't just dropping in to do the kill. You play a part.

Today I get in place just when the sun is a thin line on the eastern horizon. Have you ever tried to merge into the woods at that time of day? Have you ever listened to everything wake up out there? It's one of the most remarkable experiences a person can have. But to hear it, you got to be quiet, not just with your mouth or your body, but inside your head.

I look out on that abandoned, weeded-up subdivision—a dream gone bad just appearing one more time, one more day, out of the dark of God's night—and I see nature reclaiming it. The weeds turning green, blooming here and there, covering up what that real-estate guy tried to do. And no people anywhere. It makes me think there's hope for our world yet.

And then I hear the crows and the owls in the woods that border the abandoned subdivision lots. The crows are cawing the start of the day, arguing with one another like they always do. Crows always sound like they're pissed off about something. And nobody can find the owls. They're going to bed for the day, leaving behind a mysterious hoot or two just to leave everybody wondering about them. And then the other birds tune in—the jays and the warblers and the chickadees.

What lots of people don't know about the woods is that animals talk to one another. You have to sit and listen—concentrate, I mean—to know that. Now I don't mean that the animals talk like people. But I mean that the crow cawing out there and carrying on about this or that might provoke a hoot from an owl that's going to sleep or a gobble or two from a turkey that is just stirring around on the roost. I have no idea what these sounds mean, but I do know they mean something. They're not just background noise for people to build subdivisions by.

Once when I was small, my father took us camping way up in the Smokies. Our campsite was underneath these huge cedar trees and oaks and hickories. As we sat around the fire that night, my daddy started telling scary stories, but we all lost interest in them because of a night bird of some sort that was playing games with us.

He would call quietly from the trees on one side of the fire and then when we shined our lights in the tree to see him, he would fly off. In a few minutes he would be on the other side of the campsite. If we tried to ignore him, he would get louder and louder, come closer and closer. On and on it went as if he were playing chase with us. And we never did see him. We just heard his mysterious voice in the dark among those tall, ancient trees. Some kind of way he was communicating with us, trying to say something to us. It was then that I knew the woods were for me.

By now the sun is peeping over the horizon, and I wait. I have a crow call in my pocket. Sometimes I'll use it to locate a gobbler, get him started, but this morning I don't need it. The crows keep at it, and before long I hear a gobble or two from somewhere to my left. I look over and see a large hickory tree surrounded by pines and sycamores. I wait a respectful two minutes or so, and then I cluck a couple of times loud enough and fast enough to attract attention. Everything is quiet for a moment or two. It's as if the crows and the owls and everything else are all waiting to see what I've said. To guess what I am. And then there it is before the crows can tune back up: gobble.

I cluck again, but now I slow the tempo as if I'm being coy. It's a strange thing about gobblers. They're all different, so you have to move a step at a time and see how they react. What works on one bird won't work on another.

Gobble, gobble, gobble.

I know now that I've piqued his interest, confounded him. It's like playing a man. You do what he expects, and he'll use you. So you play hard to get. Keep him guessing. Gobblers expect the hens to find them, so you pretend you're a hen that isn't particularly interested in finding him. The gobbler can't believe that any hen would not be interested in him, so he wants to verify your lack of interest. You cluck a time or two more, and like every man that's ever lived, he's curious as hell. *I want to see this woman who's not interested in me. I want to have a look at her.*

Men have been falling into traps like this since the beginning of time. Why you think it was Eve who talked Adam into eating the apple instead of the other way around?

Now I cluck softly, almost like a purr—just a time or two, allowing him to fix on my location. And I wait. Doesn't take that long. I hear something coming my way, coming through that high grass. Now is the time for caution. You want to let him come on his own, let him think it's his idea. You can always purr again if you need to, but you don't want to make him suspicious. Just let his ego and his gonads drive him to you.

Well this mister is as spry and eager as a young colt. I can hear him beating a path to my door, hesitant at times, but steady. I assume he's young and stupid.

Still I wait, my gun in place, making my breathing as quiet as I can. Then I see him high stepping my way. Lord have mercy—it's an old tom with a long beard and a huge fantail. Old enough to know better. And him just a strutting.

Gobble.

I let him get to within twenty feet, looking this way and that for love, and then I steady my aim without moving.

A clean kill.

A beautiful bird. Enormous.

His feathers are iridescent in the early morning sun. Well, so much for the gobbler blight my brothers identified. I hoist him up by his feet and put him over my shoulder. He's so big and I'm so short that his head comes close to dragging the ground.

It's then, as I turn, that I see the walkers. They're from the subdivision over on what used to be Mama's land. They're outfitted with Nikes and exercise attire, strutting along in their high-hipped way to get their heart rates up, using the abandoned part of the subdivision that was to be as a walking track for their early morning exercise. A man and a woman in their forties or fifties. So I put the turkey down and take my hair out of my camouflaged hat, letting it flow, blond and curly, all down my back. Then I put the hat back on and cradle my Beretta in one arm and sling the turkey over my shoulder with the other. Then I set out to give our so-called neighbors a shock with my long blond hair, my face paint, my turkey carcass, and my gun.

They don't see me at first, and when they do, they do this double take. So predictable. But I keep walking toward them down what was supposed to be a street with houses on it. Now they're looking at me and trying not to gawk, and I know exactly what they're thinking. *Hunting this close to our home. My God, look at that bird. And a girl, a blond girl, not over fifteen.* Actually, I'm eighteen, but I look young because of my height.

When we pass, I make a point of looking right at them. "Morning," I say. "Lovely out, isn't it?"

"Hello," one of them says in a thin, distracted voice.

I pass them and then I look back quick 'cause I know that they'll both be trying their damnedest to crane their necks around and get one more look at the bird or me. Already planning what they're gonna tell the neighbors.

Our eyes meet one more time as they steal one more look. I hold onto their eyes before quickly looking away.

Gobble, Gobble, I think. *Just gobble me up. I ain't going nowhere. How 'bout you?*

His Mark

2012

Jacob White III

My mother's face has a windblown look. She's standing on the porch of the farmhouse looking out on the long dirt road that leads to the highway, and I can imagine her cheeks and her forehead as shaped by the wind like the worn-smooth faces of mountain rocks. Her thick, long gray hair, gathered and tied into a loose ponytail, blows back in the autumn wind, and she keeps looking out at the road as I sit in my father's rocker and watch her. She pulls her brown suede coat around her to shield her from the wind, then hugs herself, hands cupping elbows.

She's watching for the real-estate agent from town. He's coming to advise her on what to do with the farm. I look out at the road long enough to see the big black Escalade turn in and the dust gather and swell in its wake as it moves up the arterial dirt road toward the farmhouse.

It was a dry summer, followed by a dry autumn. The dust is everywhere. I can even taste it in the water—though my mother says that's my imagination. I get up and head in to go out back and sit with the dogs.

"You're not gonna stay and hear what he's got to say?" she calls after me.

"No," I say. "You can tell me about it."

The dogs and I often sit on the back gallery and watch the sun set behind the mountains that lie beyond the western edge of my family's land. The trees on the ridge beyond the pasture have begun to lose their color.

When I first got here in October, they were a riot of reddish brown and yellow gold, but now in early November, they've passed their prime, and they're fading into drab brown and falling. Too dry for them to maintain their color for very long. I like watching the trees and the sun setting behind the mountains on these evenings when the dusk steals in before you expect it, the wind kicking up fierce and cold. It reminds me I'm home.

As I look at the trees, I think of my father. "It's never far away," he used to say when we'd walk the mountain meadow in early summer, looking at the suddenly green grass and the ground boggy from spring rain. "A few months and this'll all be gone, covered up and frozen. It's never far away." He was talking about the winter, which is what the autumn winds remind me is coming. Winter here at the edge of the Smokies can be mighty cold—surprisingly cold. Furthermore November is the prime part of quail season, his favorite time of year. By winter it's almost over and too cold to really enjoy it.

But today I think of death. Dad died last month, just after I had started my second year at Columbia University in New York City. It was so unexpected that I didn't get to say good-bye. I came home for the funeral, and then when I realized that my mother was going to be left to settle up the farm business, I decided to leave school to help her sort matters out. I hope I can go back for the spring term.

It wasn't easy to do. With a full scholarship to Columbia University, I had a lot on the line. But it was the right thing to do, what with Lance in Afghanistan for a second time and all. It wasn't like he could come home and stay.

My mother has always said that we two are as different as night and day. Lance and me I mean. Five years older than I am, he was a hell-raiser, a lousy student, a half-count farmhand. And I was the model child, the younger brother who watched him make his mistakes and then decided to do the opposite. I was a superior student, a reliable helper when my father needed one, and the only hell I raised was when my brother told me he was joining the marines.

"What you wanna do that for?" I said, avoiding his eyes because of my instinctive shyness around him.

"You gon' get yourself killed over there trying to help people that don't wanna be helped. We've no business—"

"Right thing to do," he said, interrupting and not looking at me either. We've spent most of our lives not looking at one another. "Can't spend the rest of my life riding into to town to get drunk every weekend after working one more dead-end job."

"Why don't you go to school, get an education?"

"Not everybody wants to do that. Not everybody can."

Then he looked at me hard. "Besides, the marines'll send me to school when I get back. If I wanna go."

IF you get back, I thought, realizing that I didn't want him to go because I was afraid for him.

"He's got to do it," my mother told me later. "Gotta make his mark. I don't want him to go, but I see it's gotta be. It's like your father and the farm. He has to make his mark in the world some kind a way."

She put a hand on my arm as if she could sense my fear for him. "I just thank God for it 'cause I was afraid he'd never find himself. Didn't want that. Nobody did. Your father and I support him in this."

And now he's decided to make a career of it. And Dad is gone. So it appears that I am the last man standing.

I sit down in one of the Adirondack chairs on the back gallery and look at the faded brown ridge and the mountains behind it. The autumn air is clear and dry, and the sun is settling in behind a smear of thick cumulous clouds. Earlier in the day it looked like rain. It might come yet.

In an hour or so as the sun sinks below the horizon and into the evening clouds gathering behind the mountains, the sky will be a miracle. Happens every day out here when you can see the sun sink into the trees on the mountains. Being in New York City, I have missed that.

I've only been in the chair a second when I feel Annie's wet nose on my hand. I reach around and scratch behind her ears. She moves her head around nudging me with her nose, telling me to keep it up. There's no dog anywhere that loves a head massage more than Annie. Problem is she never wants you to stop.

Chin on paws, Duke watches me from the edge of the gallery right on the other side of the steps. He doesn't like massages at all, and he still hasn't gotten over me going off to college. He's wary of me. He cuts his eyes back to the tree line staring into nothingness. He can stare like that for hours. Mother thinks it's grief. He hasn't gotten over Daddy being gone. Keeps looking for him in all the familiar places and then, when he doesn't find him, stares off at nothing.

"They've had to put up with a lot of turmoil, a lot of change," my mother says. "Lance leaving, then you, and now your father. I 'spec they just miss folks, that's all."

Truth be told, there were no living creatures closer to my father than these two dogs. When my mother speaks of my father making his mark, she's speaking of the farm. He more or less pulled it back into existence, following the lead of his Uncle Isaac, a man I never knew. Daddy fought through droughts and bad markets and bovine diseases and ticks and no-count help and snow and rotten cattle prices and the demise of the family farm and scorchers and God knows what the hell else, working on it all the while as a second job. The rest of the time he was county attorney down in Sledge.

He was a tough man. Determined he was to see that the land my great-great-grandfather had chiseled out remained intact. Managed not to sell an acre in nearly forty years and even to acquire more. In his last years, he had a little money in the bank, some inheritance money from Mother's family and some money he made on stock. So he quit his job in town, and he hired Irving to do most of the cattle work. It was a small cattle operation, rarely more than five hundred cows, a few crops on the side here and there, but he took great pride in the fact that it existed, the fact that he kept it going in a time that was hard as hell on farmers.

Retirement, or semiretirement as he called it, left him more time to make his mark with these dogs—something else that he had worked at ever since he came back to run the farm after Uncle Isaac died. Daddy had trained them to hunt quail in the lower pasture and all over the rolling flatlands that make up much of the back part of the farm and that lead right up into the edge of the mountains. He had protected the ground cover for the quail, planted Egyptian wheat for them. Meanwhile, on the front side of the farm, the town was encroaching. Urban sprawl. Tentacles like kudzu. Relentless as death.

But what a remarkable thing it was to watch those dogs he trained quarter in that back twenty. They'd hit the ground running, noses down, tails wagging. Sometimes all you could see would be tails cutting through the brush.

About now I hear voices and movement inside the house. My mother is showing the agent the house. The dogs prick their ears and cock their heads, picking up the timbre of a strange voice. Annie barks and looks away as if to calculate what this means. Then she walks up and down the gallery nervously. Duke stays put, but his head is up, his nose twitching, his ears back. He pulls his jaws together and pricks his ears up, cocking his head ever so slightly to catch every nuance of the strange new sounds. Then he emits one of those guttural growls that is strangely menacing for an English setter. They're usually pretty quick to warm up to strangers. I guess they're both still wondering where Daddy went.

A few minutes later I hear car doors shut—thunk, thunk—and see the Escalade head out the dirt road that leads to the back part of the farm. My mother and the real-estate agent are looking at the rest of the spread. Both dogs bellow now, aware somehow that the vehicle they hear is not one that they know. They take off into the yard, and I watch them. They're lean and sleek from hunting and from free ranging on the place. Duke is ticked and spotted with black and Annie with orange. I keep them clean and brushed just the way my father taught me to. There are no tangles or matting in the feathering along the legs and tails. Except for the spots and the ticking, their coats are resplendently white.

They always know when something's wrong. When I first got home, they treated me like a stranger. And I guess they knew that my sudden appearance and Daddy's absence added up to something they didn't like. They'd sniff at me in a standoffish way and then restlessly walk the property as if they were trying to find something that was missing, trying to get things to go back to the way they were supposed to be.

Perhaps just like people, they have to grieve and get over it. And grieving for them is walking around and looking for what's missing or lying, chin on paws, staring into the distance. But who knows? Maybe the dogs know things we can't know. Maybe they just can't tell us.

Annie was the first to soften toward me. My father always said that you can count on women to see what's got to be done and to do it even when it hurts. Men are slow and dull witted. They need to be prodded, he'd say.

"A damn woman'll kick your ass when it needs to be kicked," he'd say, referring to my mother.

Their first date was a coon hunt when they were teenagers. Her father—my grandfather—was a coon hunter and physician if you can believe that. But he's been dead many years. According to Dad, my mother was the one who prodded a bobcat out of a tree so the hunt for coons could continue. Otherwise the dogs would have stayed focused on that damn bobcat.

"I could never get that image out of my mind," he used to say. "And since then," he'd say, "she's been prodding me to do this and that and the other."

She talked my father out of a number of rather wild ideas he had over the years, but ironically the one she didn't talk him out of was keeping the farm. When she saw he had to do it, that it was in his blood, she hunkered down and made sure it happened, pushed him in ways he needed to be pushed. According to him, she was the smart one. And now she's the one who has decided to sell the farm.

"There's no one left to run it," she tells me. "Neither one of you boys has any inclination to stay here and do what your father did. And I can hardly blame you. The family farm's a thing of the past. This land'll be an albatross hanging around your neck. And I won't let it go to rack and ruin just for sentimental reasons."

A kick in the ass, just like my father said. Something I need to hear but don't want to accept.

In a sense Annie's like my mom—practical, ready to get on with life. She keeps trying to get in the truck with me, and I know exactly what she wants me to do. She wants me to take them hunting. But I'm not ready for that yet. I have never been bird hunting without my father. The heft of that .20 gauge, the sight of those dogs with their tails high and their noses down—my God, it'll just bring back too many memories. But I sense that Annie knows that the hunting must go on, that we must prove to ourselves that we can hunt without my father. Otherwise we will never hunt again. Those are the two choices.

So here I sit more in the mind of Duke, staring at this broken world and trying somehow to hold onto what's gone.

I am remembering the day of my father's funeral. A slate-colored sky, even a little drizzle before we made it to the cemetery. And then the mound of red dirt, looking like a scar in the landscape, and the coffin and the handful of mourners with umbrellas who'd come to the graveside. And the preacher with his right hand lying flat on the coffin, holding the book up with his left hand while he reads from First Corinthians:

> We shall not all sleep, but we shall all be changed. In a moment,
> in the twinkling of an eye, at the last trump: for the trumpet shall
> sound, and the dead shall be raised incorruptible, and we shall be
> changed. For this corruptible must put on incorruption, and this
> mortal must put on immortality.

And that's when I see the two deer.

They are running, two young bucks, one a spike, crossing along behind the iron railing of the cemetery. And when they make it to the copse of trees just east of the cemetery, they stop and look back at us. Even at that distance, I can tell that their ears are twitching. I look away, and when I look back, they're gone. Still, it's enough to remind me that we're in the woods. Yes, we're burying him in the woods where the Whites have all been buried for generations.

Standing behind that simple iron fence amid graves going back to the old Cherokee great-great-grandfather whose name was actually Henry Whitebear, shortened to White, you can't see anything but woods and fields. No house. No store. Nothing but the dirt road that leads to it. That's how my great-great-grandfather wanted it.

My mother has said that she will see to it that the family cemetery is preserved. But even if it is, where will it be—behind a fence in the middle of a subdivision, near some asphalt road where cars zoom by at all hours of the night and day so there is never the silence of the cedar trees on the knoll out of sight of everything? The silence and stillness that can bring the deer to stand and stare.

By now the dusk is upon us. The sun glows amber and crimson through the gathering clouds of evening, and I see the faint ghostlike outline of the cloud-cloaked moon about forty degrees from the horizon. Perhaps we'll get some rain after all. We sure as hell need it.

The Escalade pulls up, unsettling the dogs yet again. We hear the voices. My mother's and the other voice, the strange voice that makes the dogs bark again. Then a door slams and the Escalade drives off down the front drive. I can't see it, but I imagine the red taillights glowing through the cloud of dust that trails the Escalade off our property. In a few minutes Annie and Duke settle back down.

A few moments later my mother comes out the door and sits down in the other Adirondack chair, the one that Daddy always called "your mother's chair."

"Well, it's simple enough, according to Mr. Harvey," my mother says. "Town's moving this way. Mr. Harvey—he can draw up the paperwork this week and put the place on the market."

I look at the dogs. Annie has stretched out again and seems to be going to sleep. Duke still has his eyes on the distance where the sun is falling into the mountains that line the horizon. He settles back down, chin on paws. It'll soon be dark.

"Lots of people will soon be moving this way. There'll be a call for homes, subdivisions. Should be easy to sell. Market's coming back—at least in these parts."

And here I sit, thinking that the place my great-great-grandfather made his mark, the place my Uncle Isaac and my father pulled back into existence will be a subdivision. That no one will even know that they were ever here. That they ever did all the things they did. And the quail on that back twenty, the quail he planted Egyptian wheat for, they'll be gone. They'll go the way of most of the other quail in this countryside. And the dogs, his dogs, where will they hunt?

For a moment it seems unthinkable to me that the land will bear no mark of my family, that rows and rows of houses and black asphalt streets making circles and cul-de-sacs and corners will make this place as anonymous as the inside of a motel room repeated over and over and over again by the next room and the next room and the next room and the next—all identical and anonymous.

"And the dogs," I say. "Where'll they go? Where?"

"Well, they can live with me. I'll keep that acre around the house. I might build a new house—this one's pretty old." She looks around her at the clapboard sides to this house. "And though your father kept it up very well—you know it gets harder and harder to repair."

We both are silent, thinking.

"I would never abandon your father's dogs. You know that."

"But where will they hunt?"

She's silent again as we both look at the darkening sky.

"There's public land," she says. "Other people in town still have farms. Don't they? Besides, who will be here to hunt them?"

I stand up and walk off the deck and around toward the front of the farmhouse. I look east, away from the mountain ridges and the sunset. The encroaching town lies before us slightly downhill, but it's not quite dark enough to see the electric lights below me twinkling on. For a moment the setting sun blazes through the clouds in the western sky behind me and is reflected in the luminescent clouds before me. For that moment it's as if the clouds in the east are on fire, burning red against the darkening sky.

No, Mr. Harvey's wrong, I think. *There's nothing simple about signing away my father's farm. My great-uncle's farm. My great-grandmother's farm. My great-great-grandfather's farm. Nothing at all's simple about that.*

I look back at the eastern sky, and the clouds have lost their firelike glow. The dusk moves on, darkness advancing, looming.

"Wait!" I call to my mother. "Wait!" I say as I walk back around the house while the sun sinks into the darkness of the western sky.

APPENDIX

Family Ties—White and Chapman

His name was originally Henry Whitebear, and his dark skin and hair suggested that whatever else was in his past, there was at least some Native American blood. Sometimes he said that his mother was a Creek Indian; other times he said she was Cherokee. Still other times, he said he was not sure where his family had come from, or that he and the rest of the Whitebears came from the woods and the people who lived there.

When he first appeared in the Piedmont region of South Carolina somewhere around Spartanburg, he clung to a number of strange traditions. He wore his jet-black hair long, and he practiced a strange kind of Christianity that seemed to involve a number of Native American traditions, such as referring to God as the Great Father or praying to the spirits of the animals he killed when he hunted, or even camping in the woods during most of his hunts because he wanted to know the land where the animals lived, to feel its rhythms under him when he slept. But he was a member of a Baptist church out in the country, and he regularly attended even before he married a woman of the Baptist faith.

A strikingly handsome man some six feet tall, he created quite a stir around him when he began showing up in Sledge and Yellow Bluff in the early part of the twentieth century. He would strike memorable poses: standing tall and erect beside a wagon in the last moments of an October day, staring off into the sky above the tree line or leaning against a porch post at the old dry goods store in the center of Sledge, a toothpick in his mouth. Women who saw him would carry with them the intensity of his expression or the dusklike color of his skin or the dark-as-night color of his hair or his brown eyes. Had women of that era called men beautiful, they would have used the term to describe him. And if they cared about his mixed heritage, if it had ever mattered to them, they seemed quickly to forget it

Henry Whitebear courted a number of white women in the community before he eventually settled on one with whom he raised a family. Her name was Michelle Mason, the daughter of a merchant from Spartanburg. She was one of the most beautiful women in Spartanburg, but her mercantile heritage kept her from hobnobbing with the local gentry. So she married for love, not for money or position. Still, it was about then that Henry Whitebear dropped "bear" from the family name. No one knew if this were her idea or his.

In his early days, Henry White had been a sharecropper, but his work ethic was such that by the time he married Michelle Mason in 1912, he had begun to acquire farmland along the Piedmont in the shadow of the Smoky Mountains. In those days before World War I, it was still possible to make a living cotton farming the hilly land of the South Carolina Piedmont—especially if you were a hard worker, as Henry White was. And he continued to grow cotton when he got back from service in the infantry during the War. But then a decade later, toward the end of the 1920s, cotton prices began to gyrate wildly. And each year the Piedmont was harder to farm because repeated crops of cotton had leached away all the nutrients in the soil and poor farming practices had allowed erosion to take more and more topsoil. South Carolina's prime farming land would ultimately move southeast toward the coast.

By the time the stock market crashed in 1929, the White family had decided that they could no longer make a good living farming, and Henry's son, Henry, Jr., had taken a job in town and was farming on the side. And then after the Depression, like so many other farm families in the South, the Whites learned that they could not depend solely on farming to survive. And though the land stayed in the family, the progeny of Henry

White found other ways to supplement what they made farming. In fact, they reversed the equation: they used farming to supplement the living they made elsewhere

Still, the farmland that Henry Whitebear had sharecropped for, acre by acre, had a mysterious hold on them all—as if Henry Whitebear's story of his family coming from the woods, "crawling out of the woods" he would sometimes say, were true in some strange way. That the first Jacob White, the grandson of Henry Whitebear, hunted with his grandfather might have explained the pull of the land. But the first Jacob White was killed when his own son, Jacob, Jr., was no more than three, so that there was little time for the father to pass along the importance of the woods. The grandmother who raised Jacob, Jr., rarely left the house, and she had long blamed "that damn, no good farm" for her widowhood. It had driven her husband, Henry, Jr., to drink and then ultimately to an early death, according to her. Yet when she finally thought that she could be done with the farm, which more than once she called a judgment upon her, there was always someone coming home to rescue it.

Her son Isaac lost his wife to another man and with her a good half of his heart when she got custody of the two daughters he loved more than life itself. He came home to the farm to heal himself, to find a new direction for his life. Though he never really healed, he got some measure of peace from working the land and hunting. And then in his turn Jacob White, Jr., came back despite an expensive education at Boston College and a promising career as a lawyer in a firm that would have eventually made him rich. He and his wife Angela raised their two boys there on the land that Henry Whitebear had sharecropped to buy.

The grandmother, Mattie, understood none of this desire to return to the farm. It was only five years after Jacob White, Jr. came back and rescued the farm yet again that she died in her sleep and was brought back to the farm for burial beside her husband, Henry White, Jr. One of her friends muttered at the graveside, "I guess she couldn't be shut of this place no matter what." And thus, they were all buried there—the wives, the husbands, the children, the dogs—in the very dirt that Henry Whitebear had acquired acre by acre after he walked out of the woods and began living among white people.

The Chapman family was likely of Scots-Irish origin. The family tradition was that they had always been farmers in the Piedmont. Enoch Adolphus grew cotton primarily, but he declared that his ancestors had grown indigo before cotton became profitable. "We go way back," he used to say. "Way, way back." He would look over the fields when he said this, as if he could see the place from where the family had come, the very trail they had trod to get to the farm. But the only identifiable object in the range of his gaze was a log cabin that had slowly become a hunting lodge of sorts for the men in the Chapman family to use in deer and turkey hunting. Nobody knew who made it or when it was made, only that it was well made.

"That ol' boy knew what he's doing," Enoch would drone, insisting that the first Chapman to come to South Carolina cut with an axe the cypress trees that became the walls of that cabin. Indeed, those logs were cypress and had stood the test of time though generations of hunters had been forced to re-chink the space between the logs. Looking up at the six-by-six white oak rafters in the ceiling or the hand-split cedar shake shingles on the roof, no one could doubt the craftsmanship of that first Chapman if he did indeed build the cabin. But when people asked Enoch to be specific about the builder or even when the cabin was built, he just rambled on about "what Grandma used to say."

He had a thin, high-pitched voice and he talked rapidly, chewing his words up, so it was always hard for people to know exactly what he had said. So no one was sure when the first Chapman had made the trip across the Atlantic, where that first Chapman had originally landed, or when the Chapmans had come to South Carolina to build that cabin—if indeed one of them built it. They only knew that as long as anyone could remember, there had been a Chapman on that land just out of Sledge near Spartanburg and that cabin had been there.

By the early part of the 20th century, the Chapman family members were all so occupied with trying to scrape a living from the land, that they had ceased to care about the heritage of the family. The stories that Enoch Adolphus had rattled off in his high pitched, chewed-up voice were lost amid the struggle with drought and falling cotton prices and everyday disasters, such as the tornado that swept through on April 5, 1926, and destroyed the front half of Enoch's house and his entire barn. The Chapmans and their neighbors rebuilt both within three months.

Like everyone else, the Chapmans found the 1920s and 1930s to be decades of decline as more than one family discovered that farming would not be enough to sustain even a tolerable livelihood. Thus, Enoch Adolphus, who missed the First World War because he was too old for it, stopped telling family stories and began looking forward to retiring into town. He was possessed by a great desire to be rid of the worry and the travail of trying to make money farming. Then right after World War II ended, his only daughter, Rachel, was killed along with her husband, Jacob, in a tragic automobile accident. Rachel had married the aforementioned Jacob White, the son of Henry White, Jr., who in his turn was the son of Henry White, Sr., formerly known as Henry Whitebear. Rachel and Jacob left behind them an infant son, Jacob, Jr.

This tragedy nearly killed Enoch, and his wife Gladys quickly grieved herself to death-though the official cause of her death was listed as "congestive heart failure." So Enoch, having lost a daughter and a wife in short order, split the farm between his grown sons, Edward and Nelson, and moved into Spartanburg to retire. He became one of those sad old men who sat along the town square, chewing tobacco, discussing politics, and drowsing through the long afternoon tedium. Enoch wanted to be rid of everything-the farm, the people in his life, life itself. This left the aforementioned Mattie White, the paternal grandmother (widow of Henry White, Jr.) to raise Jacob White, Jr., in whose blood the White and Chapman families were forever linked. With the tenacity and steel-like will that had gotten her through a failing farm, a failing marriage to an alcoholic husband, the Great Depression, World War II (in which both of her sons fought and survived), the death of one of those sons plus her daughter-in-law in a tragic automobile wreck, Mattie White set about raising her grandson. She did it almost entirely alone. At that time her surviving son, Isaac, lived too far away to be of much help. And the Chapmans—all of them, not just Enoch—seemed too grief struck even to look at the boy, let alone take him in. They were afraid they would see Rachel's face in his. Only Uncle Ted helped her. And he was no uncle at all—he was a cousin from her side of the family who lived in Sledge. He spent most of his time in local bars picking up women that Mattie called "disreputable." But he was close and could be depended upon in a pinch, especially if Mattie threatened to call his mother.

Nelson Chapman sold his part of the Chapman land almost as soon as Enoch bequeathed it to him. He moved to California and established a new branch of the Chapman family. If he ever came back, no one remembered or reflected upon his visit. He quite simply took the money and fled the South. But Edward passed his land on to his sons Edward, Jr. and Carl. Having gotten an education on the GI Bill, Edward, Sr., was interested in moving to Spartanburg to spend more time developing his insurance business, something that had become what he called his "day job."

It was about this time or a little later in the decade of the 1950s that Ivor Wilson came into the area. He claimed to be related to the Chapman family. His branch of the family had left the Carolinas back when the Chapmans were still growing indigo, according to Wilson. They had established themselves in Virginia. They grew a little tobacco and raised horses, but mostly worked in politics and law. They were gentleman farmers, the kind who hired out all the farm work so that they could work in town and yet still have the advantages that came with owning a farm. One of those advantages was quail hunting, something all the men in the family dearly loved. Ivor claimed that his father was a lawyer and a state senator and even ran for the United States Senate once, though he lost. He was also a crack shot and an expert dog trainer. Ivor himself was a retired professor and looked and acted like no Chapman anybody ever saw.

None of Enoch's stories, in so far as people could hear them or remember them, ever said anything about Virginia or a Wilson branch of the family. But Ivor came to town with lots of money, thanks in large part to his wealthy black friend Eric Be Lieu, also a professor from Virginia. Together they bought the old Ramsey place, a defunct cotton farm, and set about making it into "a quail plantation" of some sort—raising setters and pointers, doing field trials, protecting quail habitat. People around town did not know what to make of any of it—"a quail plantation," a rich black man, a retired professor, blacks and whites in business together.

"That ain't no Chapman," the old men that sat in Samson's Barbershop would say. "If it tis, it's the blueblood, liberal side of the family. No Chapman ever talked like that man. No Chapman ever had that kind a money or dressed like that. And no Chapman had friends like that ole Eric."

Still, lvor Wilson and his partner Eric were eventually granted a grudging acceptance because of the hunting—this despite the fact that they broke the unwritten rules of wealth and class and ignored the color line. And so over time, the Chapmans—at least those who hunted—accepted Wilson's stories of kinship and started calling him Uncle Ivory. And every autumn when quail season opened, people from Sledge would find a way to be invited quail hunting by Uncle Ivory though they were very reluctant to pay for the privilege, something that the business needed if it were going to survive. And then quail populations in the South began declining because of farming pressure, pesticides, ants, clear-cutting, hawks. This meant that there were fewer quail hunters in the area. And Eric got enough of South Carolina, what with people wanting to hunt for free and asking him if he really owned the land on which they hunted and if he didn't just work there. He sold out and left. Went back to his Chicago home. So old Uncle Ivory was left alone on his portion of the spread to train his beloved dogs, to plant Egyptian wheat, and to protect the groundcover for the quail. The so-called "quail plantation" failed.

Edward Chapman, Jr., or Eddie as he was known, the other son of Edward, Sr., felt the call to preach. He became an itinerant pastor, preaching hell and damnation in various Baptist Churches and camp meetings around the region. He also farmed the land his father had bequeathed to him, farmed it just enough to make ends meet. Neither preaching nor farming provided an adequate income, but putting them together enabled him to eat and clothe himself while pursuing his two passions rabbit hunting and saving the lost.

Then he met the love of his life, Rhonda Morris, while watching a service station attendant pump gas into his car at the Texaco station in the center of Sledge in December of 1959. At first, she demanded that he go to seminary and become "a real preacher." Because he was never keen on the idea and kept putting off applying for admission to college—he had never been any more than a poor student—she finally pursued a new solution for what she considered to be his lackluster income and his profligate laziness. Together they turned the farm into a chicken operation.

Eddie never got rich raising and selling chickens, but he did do well enough to give up the pulpit. In many ways he was primed for a new profession, for by the late 1950s, he had some theological issues, a kind of mysterious dark night of the soul that made him lose faith in the church for a time. He could have done better at chicken farming had he been willing to do what Rhonda demanded—indeed hounded him to do—and give over everything to poultry production. He came into the chicken business just when the demand for chicken "broilers" skyrocketed in the lower forty-eight, and chicken production companies contracted with farmers, providing chicks and feed in return for 12 to 16 growing weeks on the farm in long rectangular sheds covered in tin. The company then paid a pre-arranged price for each healthy bird.

But the chicken buildings compromised the quality of the hunting on his land. Nobody wanted to be downwind from those buildings-not even the rabbits, squirrel, and deer. And for that reason Eddie agreed only to house chickens on the part of the farm that was a mile or so up from the river. The canebrake area around the river and the surrounding fields and woods he protected even though it cut in on his income. Still, Chapman land in the shadow of Smokies was now dotted with long rectangular chicken buildings that emitted quite a stench as well as the constant clucking and milling around of hundreds of chickens packed wall to wall. People in Sledge wondered what that original Chapman—the one who, according to Enoch, built that well-made cabin—would have thought.

Eddie did well enough as a chicken farmer to raise two children-a boy named Lumpkin and called "Lummy" and a girl named Laura, who married into the Jones family, another Piedmont farm family. Lummy was lazy like his father, but had none of his father's ability to develop keen and absorbing interests, such as preaching or rabbit hunting. His main endeavor was watching and talking South Carolina football with his young son Wilson. Laura had all the energy that Lummy lacked, and like her mother, she was fated to marry a man who was by nature indolent. Ben Jones piddled at a number of careers before he settled on opening an auto repair shop/ tire store just outside of Spartanburg. With Laura pushing and encouraging him, Ben Jones went to work every day. But her life was short. She died of breast cancer before her children were grown, leaving Ben Jones to begin selling off piece by piece the land she had inherited as he left the running of the shop to others and struggled to raise three children alone.

The boys were fairly content with the life their father provided them, but Lauren Chapman Jones, the daughter, kept alive the dominant spirit and energy of her mother. She was a better hunter than her brothers or her father and a better student than anybody in the county—even Jacob White, III. People in Sledge predicted that when she left for college in the fall of 2011, she would never come back for anything more than a visit. Nobody had any idea of what she would do, but they figured that whatever it was, she would do it well and in the process wind up in charge of much of the known world before she was forty years of age. "She's just that smart and just that bossy," people would say.

Folks around Sledge always remarked that Eddie got the religion in the Chapman family and Carl got the love of whiskey, also a distinct strain in the Chapman line going all the way back to Scotland. A good ten to fifteen years older than Eddie, Carl married a Methodist woman named Susan. She had a stiff spine and a long-suffering disposition; otherwise, she could have never lasted with a man who was at once so demanding and so unreliable.

He farmed a little on the land Edward, Sr. had bequeathed to him. He hunted a great deal. Most of his living came from his becoming a hit or miss, amateur real estate developer. There were years when the family was flush with cash and then years when they barely scraped by. But people always knew when Carl was doing well. He bought a new truck- "top of the line, loaded" he'd brag. Then he'd start spending more and more time at the local bar or out in the field hunting quail. Then in a year or two, folks would notice that he was driving a beat up, used Ford and working hard again. Because he often needed money, he was forced to sell off portions of the land he had inherited though he did pass some of it along to his sons. Sometimes he made a killing. But other times, he essentially gave away land—his drinking made him desperate and willing to believe almost anything he heard in terms of land prices, especially if he heard it in a bar after he had thrown back several drinks.

Carl and Susan had three boys: Larrie, Johnny, and Elvin. Larrie inherited his father's near amazing hand-eye coordination as well as his love of the bottle. As a result of the former, he was one of the best bird hunters in Laurens County or Spartanburg County. But as a result of the latter, he tended to lose wives, and as he got older, he tended to miss what he was shooting at as the whiskey hurt his focus and his coordination. Both Johnny and Elvin moved away—Johnny down toward the inner coastal region of the State and Elvin to Alabama. All three boys loved to hunt just as their father had, but only Larrie was truly gifted at it. And true to form, he died trailing a deer with a flask of bourbon tucked away in his hunting clothes. His grown sons, Lonnie and Clayton, progeny of him and his second wife, found the empty flask and the deer he was tracking before they found him.

"It was a doe," they said to the coroner after they found their father's body. "Gut shot."

ABOUT THE AUTHOR

H. WILLIAM RICE is the chair of the English Department at Kennesaw State University. An avid outdoorsman, he has written stories about hunting and fishing that have appeared in a number of publications, including *Gray's Sporting Journal* and *Sporting Classics*. He is the author of two books as well as many essays on an array of subjects. *The Lost Woods* is his first book-length work of fiction.